SANDCASTLES IN RHODES

Copyright © 2024 by Raven Leithe Harlow.

All rights reserved.

No part of this publication may be reproduced, stored or transmitted in any form or by any means, electronic, mechanical, photocopying, recording, scanning, or otherwise without written permission from the publisher. It is illegal to copy this book, post it to a website, or distribute it by any other means without permission.

This novel is entirely a work of fiction. The names, characters and incidents portrayed in it are the work of the author's imagination. Any resemblance to actual persons, living or dead, events or localities is entirely coincidental.

Raven Leithe Harlow asserts the moral right to be identified as the author of this work. Raven Leithe Harlow has no responsibility for the persistence or accuracy of URLs for external or third-party Internet Websites referred to in this publication and does not guarantee that any content on such Websites is, or will remain, accurate or appropriate.

Designations used by companies to distinguish their products are often claimed as trademarks. All brand names and product names used in this book and on its cover are trade names, service marks, trademarks and registered trademarks of their respective owners. The publishers and the book are not associated with any product or vendor mentioned in this book. None of the companies referenced within the book have endorsed the book.

First edition.

Cover art by Sevennah Storm.

Editing by William Burkhart at SIXDOOM LITERARY LLC.

Trigger Warning

This book contains explicit and graphic sexual content that some readers may find offensive, including adultery and multiple partners. Also expressed in this book there are themes of death, grief and infertility which readers may find upsetting.

Please proceed with caution and prioritize your mental wellbeing. It would be recommended to skip this content if you find any of the above distressing, or ensure you have support available.

"The world is indeed full of peril, and in it, there are many dark places; but still, there is much that is fair, and though in all lands love is now mingled with grief, it grows perhaps the greater."

- J.R.R. Tolkien

One

Nico

Sandcastles. Hundreds of them, dotted across the surface of the soft sandy beach that lay at the foot of the bar. In the hazy morning sun, there were only the crumbling remnants left. Once perfectly formed, like my life, the unpredictable Grecian sea slowly ebbed away at each one, until all that was left was a pile of sand; or in my case, a pile of shit.

My sweat-drenched cotton shirt clung to me like a second skin. The day was still young, yet this heat was unrelenting. *Today is going to be too hot.* Tourists could never handle the intense heat that the Grecian Island of Rhodes offered at times, stupidly wandering around the old town, and then taking out their heat-induced crankiness on locals like myself who were trying to provide them a service.

I sighed as I continued to set up the sunbeds under the straw parasols; every single one would be full soon, the restaurant behind me would be teeming with customers. I glanced at my watch; 04:55. I seemed to be setting up earlier and earlier these days, hours before the other beachfront restaurants along this strip of the coast. Away from the thrum of the nightclubs at night, but during the day this section was flooded with hundreds of vacationers demanding ice-cold drinks and handmade ice-cream.

Every day as the anniversary of the incident neared, I slept very little. Vivid memories haunted my waking moments, while they spiraled into uncontrollable and tortuous nightmares during sleep. Last night had been no different, except I could not control the tremors that shook my body until my bones rattled. I could not clear the image in my mind of Lara and Eve's final moments.

Every year, the flashbacks become more vivid: painful reminders of my failure to protect them. *Walls of scorching and unrelenting fire. Screams of terror echoing as my fear suffocated me from behind the barricade I was being forced to stay behind. Plumes of smoke hiding the full extent of Hephaetus' wrath. Lara and Eve taking their last, gasping breaths.*

Despite the heat radiating from the hazy morning sun, a shiver rippled across my body, leaving goosebumps in its wake. Their faces flashed before my eyes, beautiful and perfect in every single way. Lara's creamy-white complexion, surrounded by her sleek, ash-blonde hair, naturally gorgeous with her blue eyes that reflected the calm skies overhead. Thin, delicate lips that revealed perfectly straight teeth when she smiled. It was that smile that I fell in love with all those years ago, the way it transformed her face and made her eyes sparkle. We had been friends since school, lovers since the age of eighteen. I knew all along she was the woman for me. The love of my life. *Lara was the only woman my heart will ever belong to.*

Lara had always wanted children. We had always assumed we would have a big family. Both of us wanted to be surrounded by the pitter-patter of small footprints and the constant babble of infants, so we were overjoyed when we welcomed Eve into our lives, two months after Lara's nineteenth birthday. Lara might have been a young mother, but she had been fantastic, a natural.

An ache of loneliness sank deeper in the pit of my stomach as I recalled Lara's patience during the night feeds and the soft lullabies she would sing to Eve as she paced our apartment trying to get her back to sleep. Eve was Lara's carbon copy, even at the age of my last memory of her, the two of them waving at me from across the beach as they headed towards the marina. Soft tendrils floating on the sea breeze as they waved and blew kisses in my direction. They were my world, my everything, until they were cruelly ripped away from this world.

I had only taken on the managing of this bar because Lara had convinced me to, rather than sell it after my father had died.

I had wanted to sell it, to be free from the burden of running a business in this unstable economic climate; but it had been Lara's persistence that had kept me holding the reins. I worked long hours during the holiday season so that I could provide for them, to ensure we could get by in the winter and save for Eve's future. Without either of them, keeping the restaurant seemed pointless yet it gave me something to focus on - a reason to keep living.

"Proinos adelfos!" A booming male voice called, pulling me back to reality. "Good Morning, brother!" My eyes snapped to the sound of his voice allowing a hint of a smile to flit across my lips at the sight of Andreas. He was my father's best friend, and had been a permanent fixture in my father's business since it first opened in the eighties. The years had not been kind to him, he was no longer a towering, ominous presence who commanded respect. Instead stood before me was a wrinkled, stooped shell of his former self. When I was a boy, Andreas taught me how to work in the kitchen, how to serve the perfect pint, and how to carry multiple plates of piping hot food without dropping a single one. Even at his age now, several years past retirement, he was still one of my first employees to arrive and the last to leave.

"Morning Andreas." I replied, setting up the last of the parasols and reached out to shake his proffered hand. He pulled me into a hug, his huge palms patting me on the shoulder. "I think we are gonna be busy," I added. "Set to be a scorcher today."

He nodded slowly as he stepped back, his blue eyes were diluted from the passing of time, his tanned complexion grew more wrinkled and stretched with each fleeting day. "That's what we want, Nico. "Let's hope we have many more of these before the close of the season."

My mouth drew into a taut line. *Don't remind me.* I hated the off-season, the months between October and March when Aphrodite's would be closed, when I would have nothing to occupy my mind in the early mornings nor keep me busy throughout the day, just long and seemingly endless days to sulk in misery.

Andreas kept my hand still in his vice-like grip. "You look tired Nico. These early mornings are no good for you. You must rest." His voice was full of concern, like that of a father. "I can take care of this place if you need to take a few days off."

I will have plenty of time to rest once I am dead.

The wind picked up, the cool salty breeze tousled my hair and billowed my shirt, catching Andreas' scrutiny. "You need to eat more Nico, before there is nothing left of you." He scowled, "I will make us some breakfast." I watched his form disappear into the dark restaurant, flicking the lights on in his wake including the neon-sign: Aphrodite's.

I exhaled deeply, my attention fixed on the sign, hearing the faint thrum of electrical power generating it. It was the original sign my father had first opened up with, one of the few things he refused to change. My father was proud of this place, it had become one of the largest and most popular restaurants in Rhodes, the first of them all to open along this stretch of the beach, offering a free sunbed to all customers. Over the years, many popped up further along this stretch, but our competitors never made a dent in our trade. Families and honeymooners preferred the characteristic and authentic charm Aphrodite's restaurant and bar held rather than the glass and chrome, impersonal and modern designs of the others.

Named after the goddess of love, my parents used to run it together - a labor of love. The three of them: Father, Mama and Andreas used to work dawn until dusk until the profits began to roll in with the increasing tourism trade. Now I had a handful of servers and kitchen staff, yet I preferred to do as much hard graft myself, just to occupy my thoughts from wandering to the tragic day that changed me forever.

There was only one real perk from being a bachelor of a highly respectable establishment: the women. I could never replace what Lara and I once had, nor did I want to. But a man still had needs that the right hand could only satisfy to a certain degree. I did not want to admit how many one-night stands I've had with the female tourists who frequented this place. There was never a greater distraction than being buried between the thighs of a voluptuous woman. They all seemed to lose their inhibitions the moment their feet stepped onto the Greek soil. Perhaps it was the blazing sun, the freedom from the monotony of life back home, or the gentle whispers of the waves as they lapped at the shore that made these women so aroused.

I thought back to the woman from last night, a red-headed English woman vacationing with her family; her husband and three children. I felt no shame or remorse for fucking her here on my secluded and fenced private beach, for enjoying her mouth wrap around my cock as I thrust it deep into her throat before releasing my warm load for her to swallow. Not once did I question what excuse she made up to her husband so she could sneak out to meet me. She was a willing participant; her adulterous actions were her problem, not mine.

It was the only way I knew how to cope - shutting my emotions off and keeping myself busy with work and women. The first year was the hardest, seeing couples choose Aphrodite's beach as the romantic setting to propose or celebrate their honeymoon because of the idyllic views of crystal-clear waters and cloudless skies. Fools hopelessly in love and under the notion that they were destined for each other - soulmates. Each couple set on making grand gestures and extravagant displays of public affection, yet each one was a carbon copy of the last - so predictable, so mind-numbingly unimaginative it was almost humorous. Every one of them brainwashed, believing that nothing could take away their happiness, that the world only revolved around them. Now I see their actions as nothing more than a scene from a soppy chick-flick Lara used to love. All of them were pathetic and naïve.

Yet what hurt the most was going home to an empty apartment, not seeing their eager faces waiting for my arrival, not kissing Lara, and hugging my daughter after a long day of arduous work. All that waited for me now were the ghosts of all that I once had lurking in the darkness.

Andreas always told me that time was a healer, and I had believed him. I knew he had suffered great losses over the years, but he had never had to bury his wife or child. All that time had done was allow my grief and self-loathing to solidify my heart until it was as hard as stone.

I tried to convince myself that living this bachelor life in my mid-thirties suited me; that I was happy to have no responsibilities other than Aphrodite's to care about. Yet the truth was I wanted my old life back; my wife and my daughter. I would have done anything, sacrificed everything, in a heartbeat if I was given that chance. But it did not matter how much I wanted them, they were gone. I would never have the opportunity to be happy again.

"Nico!" Andreas' voice called from the open restaurant door, his frantic gesture for me to come inside. "Come and eat while it's still hot!" he hollered. I gazed across at the crumbling sandcastles scattered along the beach once more before turning my back on them. The pain of the seventh-year anniversary that loomed tomorrow was too heavy a burden to bear. I had not felt hungry until I caught the scent of Andreas' scrambled eggs and fried bacon, instantly making my mouth salivate and my stomach rumble.

Two plates of delicious food and two steaming mugs of coffee sat on the table closest to the kitchen. The atmosphere was heavy and tense as we ate in silence. I chose to look around at the decor, noting that the earthy tones of beige and browns needed a fresh lick of paint and the ceiling was starting to yellow from the cigarette smoke that used to linger thick and dense in the air. I decided during the off season I would renovate the place, keeping it light and airy while still complimenting the natural stone brickwork and dark oak tables. *Perhaps I may even revarnish the tables and buff the floor.*

The sudden clatter of metal against the porcelain plate pierced the silence. "Nico, don't you think it's time you moved on?" Andreas said finally, his gaze focused intently on me. "Rather than diverting all of your energy solely into this place?"

I thought about it for a moment before shaking my head; it was not the fact that I refused to move on, it was physically impossible for me to do so. Other than Andreas and my business, I no longer had any interest in anything or anyone, no matter how hard they tried.

Two

Cali - *three days ago.*

My mother once told me that rain on your wedding day was a bad omen, a sign that this marriage was not meant to be. My eyes watched the gloomy, gray sky beyond the tall, arched windows, hearing the rain lash heavily against the glass. *Everything is going to be fine, it's just a silly superstition. Adam is the one, he will always be the one.*

My gaze shifted to the full-length mirror before me, barely recognizing the woman staring back at me. Not only had the hair and make-up stylist done a fantastic job covering my imperfections, but also the dark rings that circled my tired and weary eyes. Sleep had evaded me last night, unrelenting doubts that something was going to ruin the wedding had plagued my dreams.

The woman before me showed a collected calm in her poise and an elegance in her demeanor which was the complete opposite to how I felt inside. Beneath the composure, my stomach was a mass of knots.

The slender ivory dress bore no frills or lace, just a simple silk that clung to my body like a second skin, hugging my curves and accentuating my toned body. My unruly mahogany curls twisted intricately into braids before being pinned to the base of my skull in a chignon bun. I looked like I had just stepped out of a page in a bridal magazine. The bridal suite's classic wooden panel walls surrounded me, capturing the essence of the glossy pages I had pored over for months planning this occasion. The moment Adam and I had seen this church in person, seeing the elegant gothic-era details, we knew instantly this was where we were going to get married, no matter the cost.

Glancing around at my surroundings, in a vain attempt to distract my anxious mind, I spotted every miniscule detail that most would not notice at a quick glance. Small poppies were hand carved in all of the dark wood furniture, each piece matching from the full-length mirror to the chairs on either side. One of which my maid of honor had been sitting in minutes ago.

The time was nearly here, the moment I have been planning for almost a year, to pledge my marital vows to the man who I loved; the man I wanted to spend the rest of my life with. I thought back to the day we first met, it had been the first of October, and not dissimilar to today. The floodgates of heaven had been opened; unleashing a relentless assault of torrential rain that battered against the window with no signs of stopping.

I had just finished college and was waiting at the bus stop, huddled under the hood of my coat, and clutching my backpack to my chest trying to save my books inside from being soaked and ruined. When suddenly a large black umbrella was held over my head, he appeared out of nowhere, his face perfectly composed; not even a flicker of emotion as he ran his free hand through his blond hair. I had mumbled a thanks and we had exchanged very few words. When the bus turned up, we parted ways as strangers once more. Yet day after day, we would bump into each other, it had become almost a ritual, and on the days he was not there, I found myself missing our awkward interactions. It had taken me almost two months to strike up a real conversation with him, learning that he had recently started a new job near my college and that he was almost six years my senior. We started getting off a few stops earlier and having dinner together before heading home and less than a month later we were officially dating. It was a slow and steady relationship which became more and more intense and serious as the months passed by. *And here we are now eight years later finally tying the knot!*

A shiver rippled along my spine as the nervousness crept up on me once more. I had not heard him arrive and I was starting to panic. The large grandfather clock showed that the ceremony should have already started. *Everything will be fine, he isn't that late, it must be the weather.*

Through the slight crack left in the door by my maid of honor Stephanie, I could hear voices in the hall. I instantly recognized the voice; Adam's best man and brother Craig. "How can Adam be late for the most important day of his life?" I did not catch the other person's muttered response.

I could feel my pulse quicken and my palms growing damp with sweat. *What if something has happened to him? What if there is something wrong?* Not even the deep breathing technique was helping steady my frazzled nerves. Tears were stinging the corners of my eyes but I refused to let them fall. *I had not paid so much for my make-up to ruin it by unnecessary tears.*

Hushed whispers and hurried footsteps resonated louder than before, only catching small snippets of conversation, relaxing a little at the sound of Adam's dulcet tones. "Yeah, I know... they can wait a little longer... I just need a few minutes..."

I heard his shoes thump along the stone floor past my door, stopping momentarily outside my door. "Adam..." Stephanie's voice hissed, before his footsteps resumed further down the hall closely followed by the hurried clicking of her stiletto heels. The heavy oak door of the groom's suite slammed shut. I sighed, trying to relish in the relief that Adam was here, yet the grandfather clock ticked loudly as several more minutes passed by. *What is going on? Why haven't I been called for the start of the ceremony?*

The silence was deafening. No movement, no sounds, no one was coming to get me. *But Adam's here!* Before I realized what I was doing I had already made my way down the hall to his suite, the tradition of not seeing each other until we were face-to-face at the altar completely abandoned. I had that gut feeling something was wrong. *Was it my mom?*

My hands trembled as I reached for the handle, unsure what to think or what to feel. *Today should be the happiest day of my life.* I shook my head, trying to tell myself I was being silly. *nothing is wrong, I have just missed him.* It had been three days since I last saw him, waving him goodbye when his brother came to whisk him away to Ibiza for his bachelor's weekend. Adam had called the moment they had landed; his voice slightly slurred as he spoke, as he claimed he loved me and could not wait to make me Mrs. Calista Roberts.

I longed to be near him, to feel the warmth of his body against me in his reassuring embrace and to see his handsome smile. The door opened silently; my heartbeat throbbed in my ears as I stepped inside.

The sound of their muffled voices filled my ears, catching fragments of their disjointed conversation. "I was worried you weren't going to show up..." Steph's voice sounded.

"Steph, I can't do this..."

"You need to... Cali can never find out."

"Fuck! Steph... I can't do this anymore..."

As I stepped further into the room, my blood froze and my body became paralyzed as I took in the scene before me. My mind was unable to fully comprehend what I was witnessing. His hands on her body. They were kissing, deep and passionate kisses, their eyes closed, unaware I was even in the room. Steph gasped for breath as she broke apart from their kiss, "You are here now... you have to go through with this."

"No, Steph. I don't. We could leave. Right now." Adam sighed. "I thought I could... I thought by coming here and going through with it, my feelings would change." He ran his hand through his hair, his face showed a flicker of emotion for the first time. "I can't do it... just to make *her* happy."

My heart shattered into a million pieces.

"Adam... fuck... this is so wrong." Steph's head was resting in the crook of his neck, hiding her face from my view. "We should never have let this happen..."

I continued to watch in horror as Adam's arms tightened around her waist, pulling her body closer and his mouth close to her ear.

His hands cupped her face as he pressed his forehead against hers. His shoulders sagged. "Steph, I don't want to skulk around anymore..."

My eyes watched their entangled bodies, their hands caressing one another tenderly. I could not recall the last time Adam had held me that way or shown me the love and affection he displayed to Stephanie now.

All of the air had been squeezed out as if my lungs were held in a vice-like grip as I watched Adam press himself up against my best friend on the oak desk, hearing it creak and groan as he pinned her against it. "Steph... after what you told me last night... how can you expect me to marry her?"

"You *have* to," she breathed.

Their meeting was suddenly interrupted by the chiming bells of the church, the final call for the bride and groom to meet at the altar. It startled me and snapped both of them back to reality. That was when Stephanie's eyes noticed me standing there. Her eyes widened and her body tensed.

"Shit." She hissed, wriggling free from his grasp. Regret and shame flashed across her pale face, her slate gray eyes brimming with tears. "Cali, I can explain!" she yelped, rushing towards me. I wanted to move but my feet were rooted to the spot.

"Cali..." she pleaded, clutching at my wrists, her gaze begging for forgiveness. I yanked them free from her grasp, my eyes narrowing as they flitted between the two of them.

Steph's tears left long black trails in her mascara. "Cali, I-"

She reached for my hands once more. I took a step backwards. "Don't fucking touch me!" I cried, shaking my head as my own tears began to fall, blurring my vision. Ice-cold bitterness washed over me as the realization dawned on me that Adam had not been alone in the hotel room last night when he was pledging his undying love for me over the phone.

My stomach churned as a wave of nausea hit, *how long has this affair been going on?* I did not hang around to ask, the walls were closing in on me, suffocating me. Hurt, betrayed and humiliated on what should have been the most special and important day of my life. *I need to get out of here. I need to get away from them.*

I stared at Adam through my tears. His chiseled jaw was clenched and his mouth was sealed into a firm line. There was no remorse in him unlike Stephanie who slumped to her knees at my feet, whispering her pleas for forgiveness.

I opened my mouth to speak but no words came out. Turning on my heel, I ran, the stiletto heels clicking as I sped through the marble corridor. My pulse throbbed loudly in my ears. Refusing to look back, I barged through the double doors. Their solid mass sent a shooting pain along my right shoulder as it swung open on its hinges. Neither of them followed me yet I did not slow down until I put even more distance between myself and them as possible.

Images of them flashing through my mind as I fled along the gravel path. My thoughts procured the way Adam had been with me over the past few months; more distant and less intimate. I thought it was because I had been so preoccupied with the deterioration of my mother's health. Stupidly, I thought that Stephanie had volunteered to take over the final arrangements for the wedding out of the love we had for one another.

Our friendship started in college; we were inseparable, practically joined at the hip. We told each other *everything*, we knew everything about one another - or so I had thought.

Not once had the thought crossed my mind that either of them would form an illicit relationship behind my back while my mom was slowly dying in the hospital. Yet that was exactly what they had done. Pain tore through me as though my chest had been slashed at by monstrous claws.

Adam does not love me. Adam does not want me.

My stiletto snagged on the loose gravel and I tumbled onto the drive.

Everyone I love is lying to me. Everything is gone. I am alone.

Three

Nico

The sun was fixed at its highest point in the sky. Its unshielded rays bore down on the earth below it without remorse forcing everyone to seek respite indoors.

The thrum of chatter filled the air and the stifling heat made the restaurant seem too small and too crowded. Before me was a sea of smiling faces, yet all of my attention was fixed on the woman before me. Although it was only midday, she had already downed three cocktails and two tequila shots. Catching my eye, she removed herself from the group of girls she had entered with. *She wants to leave with me.*

I smirked, fixating on the lime green bikini she was wearing as she flirted unashamedly while leaning over the bar. Her outfit left very little to my imagination as her elongated legs stretched behind her, her ass round and juicy. "I'm a glamor model." She whispered in my ear. "I'm here for my job." I nodded, my concentration now fixed on her cleavage that threatened to burst from the small triangles of fabric that barely covered her large tits. They were fake of course, as was most aspects of her physical appearance; from the eyelashes and nails to her hair and her bronzed tan. Yet I still enjoyed staring at her, imagining burying my head between those breasts or between those long, slender legs of hers.

I may be widowed, but I still had needs. I was not looking for love, just a release from the pent-up arousal this woman stirred within. My cock was rigid with an urgent desire as I fantasized about her lips around my shaft rather than the plastic straw in her drink. Swirling her tongue around the tip of the straw, she was teasing me with an artless show of her oral prowess. She knew exactly what she was doing, her eyes dropping to my crotch, knowing her plan was working. She sucked on the straw, drawing in her cheeks and keeping her eyes locked with mine.

"So... what do you say... *Nico.*"

"Not tonight." I replied, tugging at my erection as it tried to burrow its way through the zipper of my cargo shorts.

Her movements were provocative, intentionally teasing to see if I would rise to the bait. I shook my head again, trying to ignore the way she leaned in further, resting her elbows on the countertop, squeezing the sides of her thick breasts between her arms and pushing her cleavage out. I never accepted their advances on their first day; past experiences had taught me better than to lead them on at the very start of their vacation. If I caved into my carnal urges, it would be at the very end, leaving no time for any of them to develop feelings that I could never reciprocate.

"Perhaps another time?" I smirked, my eyebrows raised in question. *How much does she really want to fuck me?* I wondered as I watched the fire in her eyes burn brighter and her lips spread wide into a smile revealing her flawless straight white teeth.

"Yeah, that would be nice." she mused, her tongue dancing around her straw once more. "I hear the sea is enchanting under the moonlight." My shaft twitched at the idea, knowing she would be too busy to give a shit about how the beach looked at night.

She raised her empty glass, signaling for another. I was happy to oblige, not only could I continue to envision her mouth sucking on something other than her straw but I was also more than happy for her to keep spending over ten euros on each cocktail she drank. "I will hold you to that, Nico." The woman said, her fingertips brushing the back of my hand as I placed a new Pina Colada before her.

"Hannah... we are going to hit another bar... you coming?" a girl barely looking eighteen said, her bleached blonde hair falling into her face. In two huge gulps the woman before me swallowed her drink, I watched as her throat moved, swallowing the contents effortlessly, feeling my need to see her do that with my seed.

She flashed a look at me, almost as if she had read my mind. "I will see you later Nico..." she smiled, backing away from the bar and rejoining her group of friends. She blew me a kiss over her shoulder as she left. My eyes followed her like a moth attracted to the bright fire that danced inside of her.

I let out a sigh of relief mixed with disappointment when she was finally whisked away by her group of friends who were similarly intoxicated.

"I will see you later." Those words haunted me, Lara's last words she had ever said to me. I tried not to dwell on it, chugging at my bottle of ice-cold water, but it tasted sour in the back of my throat. *Lara and Eve are gone, forever. No amount of one-night stands will ever ease that pain.*

Guilt flooded my mind, I had not visited their memorial site for some time, I could not bring myself to visit too often. Not because I refused to remember them, but because it evoked a fresh wave of sorrow, making their deaths more final, more real. I knew they were not there; the graves were purely monuments to signify the finality of their demise. Their towering headstones concreted the fact I would never see their smiling faces again. They were forever lost to the watery depths. Even seven years after the fact, the pain of their loss tore my insides apart.

Three nights later, basked in the iridescent glow of the full moon on the deserted beach I finally got my release. Her knees were spread in the sand, my cock buried deep in her ass, as her slit devoured her fingers greedily. She fucked like a pornstar, and when she came it was like a dam had burst soaking the sand beneath us. My name echoed on the cool sea breeze in the moments that followed her scream of ecstasy.

I preferred it this way, rather than face-to-face. No eye contact. No kissing. By fucking her from behind, her ass in the air and face close to the soft sand, it was easy to pretend she was Lara. It was what I did with all the women that had followed since her death. I was not betraying Lara's memory if I pretended they were her.

It suited me, the comings and goings of unimportant women I would never see again. The meaningless, lustrous escapades were just a release of my carnal desires, I cared not for serious relationships. I had no interest in replacing Lara. I knew nothing or no one would make me as happy as my wife and daughter, Eve, once did.

A stab of guilt and longing hit me square in the chest. I pulled out of her abruptly, her body quaked in the aftermath of her orgasm, her ass was red and raw; a huge gaping hole after being rammed by my full eight inches. I clutched her ass, spreading it wide so that I could admire my handiwork - stretching her once tight entrance and filling it with my cum and watching as the sticky white mess oozed out of her. It had been over a week since my last release, I refused to use my right hand when there were plenty of women willing to offer themselves to me. This woman was no better, though the three days of anticipation had been agony for me too.

"Ouch, Nico!" She hissed, jerking her ass out of my grasp, clenching her ass cheeks together as more of my load seeped out of her. "There is no need to be so rough *afterwards.*"

I got to my feet, rearranging my manhood back into my shorts, my eyes cast to the horizon trying to suppress the images of the incident that were permanently etched into my mind.

Walls of fire and thick black plumes of smoke. The evening sky streaked with violent reds as the destruction glowed amber below. Arms wrapped around me like a boa constrictor wrapped around me, suffocating me, stopping me from getting any closer to them. Despair flowed through my body as I helplessly witnessed the demise of my entire world.

I sighed. The sea was calm now, gentle waves rippled on the surface and lazily lapped at my feet. *They are out there somewhere.* My wife and daughter, their watery graves shared with a hundred and fifty others. All victims to one of the worst tragedies to have ever happened on the Grecian coast.

I always felt closer to them here, standing at the coastline, gazing out across the open waters, than when I visited their memorial site. After closing down for the evening at Aphrodite's, I wandered up to the graveyard, to the small and secluded spot dedicated to all those who had lost their lives on that tragic day. All that was there were two small slate plaques with their names engraved in gold script along with their dates of birth and the date of their death. The plaques were cool beneath my fingertips as they ran along both of their names, hovering over Eve's, she was the youngest among the dead. Tears slid down my face as I placed Lara's favorite flowers; white and pink lilies at the foot of the memorial feature. Seven of them for both of my girls, one lily for each year that has passed. There was not a day that passed that I did not think of them, miss them, wish that they were still here, yet I struggled to bring myself here often, the cold and emptiness and impersonal plaques helped others, but made me feel more disconnected from them.

Arms suddenly snaked around my waist startling me out of my reveries as her lips brushed against my neck. For a few moments I almost believed it was Lara - it was something of a signature move from my late wife. But the stark reality hit me like a punch to the gut as I snapped back to the present. The woman behind me, whose name I had already forgotten, was not Lara. She could never be Lara. *No woman could ever replace her.* I side-stepped out of her reach, evading her attempted caresses. Our encounter was over, I had no further obligation to this woman; I had nothing more I wanted from her.

"My flight leaves in an hour," she said, her voice a solemn lament. I gave her a small, curt nod.

"I guess this is goodbye then." I retorted, keeping my back to her, feeling the air around us change. "Have a safe journey," I added coolly, still not looking in her direction. I knew I was being a dick, ignoring the woman who I fucked moments ago, but it was the only way I knew how to get them to leave without another word, and without hope of a long-distance relationship suddenly blossoming. It was only when I no longer felt her presence behind me that I eventually glanced over my shoulder.

Sandcastles, a dozen of them, still scattered the beach slowly crumbling under the weight of gravity. Soon the tide will devour them chunk by chunk with its destructive tendrils.

A shiver ran along my spine and the hairs on the back of my neck stood on end, snapping me back to reality from my memories. It was pitch black now, the air thick and ominous, I had not realized how long I had been standing in my trance-like state watching the ripple of the tide. Almost two hours had passed, and I had not noticed a single minute slip by me.

I felt eyes on me, watching me from all angles, even though the beach was empty beach and beachfront deserted. An oppressive sensation squeezed my lungs - it was their tormented spirits surrounding me once again.

I took a casual stroll back to my apartment, no longer finding solace in their haunting company. Each step was laden with remorse, regret for not being able to save them, for not being with them at the end of their lives.

The saltiness of my tears lingered on my lips as I reached my apartment, knowing nothing waited for me inside. It was only once the door clicked shut and the darkness fully consumed me did their ghosts fully disappear among the shadows.

I crawled into my bed, sore and aching from the long day of work. The black void swallowed me whole; the silence smothered my thoughts and the darkness washed away the images of Lara and Eve from my mind. I breathed a sigh of relief as the vice-like grip they held on my heart eased.

Four

Cali *- two days ago.*

The motel's bed was hard and lumpy and the sheets smelled musty and old, much like everything else in this motel. With paper-thin walls I had heard every thrust and moan from the couple in the room next door, unable to distract my mind, envisioning the couple next door to be Adam and Stephanie, their sordid affair plagued my mind and sleep evaded me.

Hours before, when I hailed a cab from the church, the cab driver had looked perplexed. His eyes scanned my wedding dress, my mascara-stained face, his mouth pulled into a taut line. I was thankful that he did not pry, as he silently waited for me to gather up some belongings from mine and Adam's house before heading to the motel.

There was no way I could have stayed in this house, not after the disastrous wedding, especially knowing that the pair of them had defiled our bed, defiled the sacred space that had once been our home. As I scoured the place for my belongings, I thought about the late nights she had spent around my house, the pair of them supposedly planning my perfect day so that I could take care of my dying mother. Bile crept into my mouth at the thought of their coercion to keep the ceremony on track. A ruse to hide their infidelity.

I had thought of postponing the wedding because I was too preoccupied caring for my mother, but they had lured me into a false sense of security; pretending to have my best interests at heart, while they fucked behind my back. *What did I do to deserve this?*

I did not look back at the house that continued their lies and adulterous acts, feeling betrayed by it as much as by them. There had never been any signs, no clues of Adam's dishonesty. I wished I had been more perceptive, but I had been too focused on ensuring the last few months my mother had to live were comfortable and that she was rarely alone. That had always been my mom's fear, to die in an unfamiliar place all alone.

A shiver ran along my spine as I dragged myself out of the rigid motel bed, unsteady on my feet, and looked around at the cheap motel room. The peeling wallpaper was yellowed and the carpet beneath my feet was threadbare. I half-expected to see the place teeming with cockroaches, but thankfully I only saw the odd dead one curled up in the corner of the bathroom.

I splashed my face with cold water, hoping the chill would ease my itchy, bloodshot eyes, the skin beneath them swollen and sore from crying until I had run out of tears last night. I stared at my reflection in the scratched vintage mirror that hung above the basin. *I am a mess.* I scrubbed with my fingertips, removing the make-up residue until my skin was red raw and my fingers shriveled into the bumpy and wrinkled texture of prunes.

Behind me, my wedding dress was discarded like trash beside the dead cockroach. The intricate lace on the bodice was torn, the soft satin bore a thousand creases. I had shed it like a second skin last night, wanting the memories of that moment to peel away with it. I forced myself into the shower, willing the weak streams of water to wash the pain and deceit away. The tepid water drizzled like rain, cascading down my naked body, feeling the loneliness swell within. Recalling last night, feeling like a stranger in my own home as I packed a few belongings into a small suitcase.

Photographs that once stood proudly on the mantelpiece had been taken down and stored in a box in the wardrobe. Little by little my feminine touches like the scatter cushions on our bed had been removed. *I guess they had hindered their sordid trysts.*

Even as I dressed, images of the house I no longer recognized taunted me. *How had I been so stupid? How had I not seen this coming?* It was clear that I was not enough for him, that he had checked out of this relationship. *So why had he continued to string me along up until our wedding day?*

The whole time I was at the house, I was scared that Adam, or worse, both of them, would return. I did not want to face them. I wanted answers, but was not ready to talk to either of them, not ready to confront the deceit and lies they had spun for the duration of their affair. The mere thought of either of them being in the same room as me made my palms sweat and my skin crawl.

Still, I found myself lingering as my mind conjured images of their trysts in every room of the house. My imagination formulating visions of them stealing kisses on my couch while they organized the guest list and fucking on the kitchen island after taste-testing wedding cake samples. The worst was the thought of them desecrating our king-size bed where I had slept every night blissfully unaware of their betrayal.

It was in our bedroom on Adam's bedside unit that our passports and the tickets to Rhodes glared up at me - the trip that was supposed to be our honeymoon. *Would he take Stephanie instead of me?* Anger bubbled inside as I snatched up my ticket and passport, before retrieving my important documents from our safe. *Over my dead body.*

I clutched onto the ticket in my trembling hand as I slumped back onto the motel bed, remembering when we had booked the trip. Trying to incorporate visiting my estranged uncle who was unable to make it to my wedding. I had not seen him since I was a child. *Would he even recognize me now?*

We always used to visit during summer break so I never understood why our visits to see Uncle grew less frequent over the years until we suddenly stopped going all together. I knew my mom and uncle argued, I thought that was natural with siblings, though I did not know if this was true considering I was an only child. I had been thirteen when we last vacationed there, in my eyes it had been a good trip. My father made jokes about me being 'too old' to build sandcastles with him and being very protective of my choice in my outfits I wore.

So naturally I was shocked when we returned back home to hear my mom sob and vow never to return. It was not until the following year when I persisted to ask why we were not going, envious of my friends going on their vacations, that my father had revealed the truth. *"Your uncle doesn't approve of me, an American, marrying your mother Cali, and he certainly does not like the westernized culture you have been brought up around. We are not going because it upsets your mother too much to hear his hateful words."* My father had replied in a delicate and soft contrast to my fiery outburst. I never brought it up again and soon it was almost as though Uncle never existed.

That was until mother became ill, it was my idea to try and rekindle their relationship, I had not even told my mom I had invited him to my wedding, nor that as I had expected he had declined.

When I took the ticket, I had no intention of actually using it, my sole purpose was to thwart any plans Steph or Adam had of using it for themselves. Yet hours later I found myself sitting in the airport lobby carrying nothing but my handbag and a few possessions in my suitcase, waiting to board the plane.

It has been years since I had stepped foot in an airport, and even longer since I had done so alone. I found myself cowering, my senses overloaded by the roar of people, the clatter of their shoes, and the echoes of the regimented chaos inside the departure lounge made my temple throb in agony.

Everyone here seemed to be happily engaged in conversation, eager to depart on their vacations with their family or friends. Yet I sat here alone, solemn, keeping my focus on the gate information boards to avoid any awkward glances or stilted conversations. Occasionally, I would glance at my cell phone, trying to resist the urge to open the several text messages from Stephanie and refusing to return her numerous missed calls. A sharp pain pierced my heart, not a single message or call from the asshole who had professed his undying love for me less than forty-eight hours ago. Curiosity overcame me as I clicked open her latest message, a plea for forgiveness, begging me to let her explain.

'There is nothing to explain,' I typed, *'you fucked my fiancé and betrayed my trust.'* My thumb hovered over the send button for a few moments contemplating whether I should send it. My anger got the better of me, furiously hitting the send button after adding *'you are both dead to me.'*

She responded immediately, but I did not read it. Instead, I scrolled through the hundreds of photos I had saved. Hundreds of memories of happier times that the three of us had once shared. Hatred seared through my veins, my hands shook in anger as I stared at them, especially at the most recent one taken three days ago. The three of us sat on the couch, ready to watch a film as we always did every Friday night when Steph did not have other plans, or if Adam was not working late. It had been a tradition we shared for as long as Steph and I had been friends. It was a much needed jovial and carefree evening so I could not resist taking some photos of us all. Now as I looked at them bile rose in my throat.

'Do you wish to delete?' My cell asked me when I hit the trash button. *Yes.* I held my breath until every last one of them was gone. *If only it was that easy to erase memories imprinted in my brain.* I could never forgive them, especially not her. She had broken my trust beyond repair. Nothing she could do or say would ever change that. The phone buzzed in my hands. It startled me, my hands were not holding the cell tight enough, so it slipped from my grasp and fell to the floor by my feet. The screen shattered on impact, but I could still make out her name in the fractured glass. I stomped on it not once, but twice. Finishing the job by discarding it in the closest trash can. *Fuck off, bitch.*

"This is the last call for all passengers for Flight 3782 to Rhodes. Gate 8 is closing in five minutes." I glanced at the digital clock on the wall, I had been so absorbed in destroying eight years' worth of memories that I had completely lost track of time. I scurried to the gate, thankfully boarding with less than two minutes to spare.

The flight attendant looked less than impressed at my late arrival. Everyone's eyes followed me as I walked down the aisle to my seat. *This was not the aisle I had been hoping to walk.* My chest tightened as anxiety gripped me. The plane was full, bar the one empty seat beside me.

The flight attendant's eyes narrowed. "Are we waiting for anyone else?" she asked in a clipped tone. My mouth tightened into a taut line as I tried not to let my bottom lip quiver. I could feel my sobs swelling in my chest. I moved my head slowly from side to side. *Please, go away.*

She must have noticed my upset as her face softened slightly. "We will be coming down with the drinks trolley once we are in the air. It looks like you need one." I gave her a curt nod before looking out the window. *There was not enough alcohol on board the plane that would help me forget.*

I gazed out of the small oval window, watching as the plane careered along the runway and up into the skies. The world beyond growing smaller as we ascended higher into the gloomy gray clouds. *What if I had not caught them, would I be on this plane now with Adam? Would he have gone along with the wedding, pretending that he actually gave a fuck about me?*

My stomach churned as I imagined being married to him while he still continued his affair with Stephanie behind my back. *Would I have ever known the truth that he no longer loved me, but her, my best friend?*

True to her word, the air hostess brought down the drinks trolley, offering me an abundance of wines and liquors. I shook my head; I had not touched alcohol since meeting Adam. "Can I have a coke please?" I asked. She nodded, handing me an ice-cold can, and holding the card machine out to me. I waited for it to beep, to confirm it had registered before cracking open the can, relishing in the sugary, syrupy liquid as it filled my mouth.

I rummaged through my handbag, pulling out the paperback I had been reading to my mom - a soppy romance where the guy finds the girl of his dreams but she refuses to succumb to his charms until he is involved in a crash and his life hangs in the balance.

I tried to read it, but not only was it far from my preferred genre of crime and thrillers, it hit home that the idea of love was all but a lie. *Our relationship had been a lie.* My mind wandered back to the house Adam and I had shared.

It had been our dream home, a typical suburban house complete with white picket fencing, located in a very desirable location: close to the schools we had envisioned our children attending, and close to Adam's work. Adam liked it because the house was spacious and modern in design with large panes of glass that spanned from floor to ceiling and allowed natural light to flood into each room, giving it a spacious and airy feel. He felt it was perfect to raise a family and all I wanted to do was make him happy.

Adam yearned for a family of his own, especially after the upbringing he and his brother had. Ferried between various foster homes after being brought into the world by addicts for parents, neither of them had ever truly been shown love and affection. Adam longed to be a father, a good one, to fill this home of ours with the patter of children's footsteps. His dream to give his future children the childhood he had been deprived of. I wanted to make that dream a reality for him, and for years we tried, but ultimately I failed him. Every time my period came, bright red and heavy, was another slap to the face. Each time it had become harder for Adam to suppress his disappointment and sadness. Until one day we agreed to undergo various tests. They had found no issues on his end; his sperm was healthy and his count was high - the problem lay with me and my eggs.

We began IVF treatment and even discussed surrogacy or adoption, but with my mother's sudden decline in health, starting a family had to be put on hold. *Was that the reason he stopped loving me?*

I looked out of the window as the scenery beyond the small window began to take form with the plane's descent. Trees sprouted leafy branches from the green blur they had once been and buildings became more distinguishable from the gray shapeless blobs from afar. A world full of vibrant colors and life beyond the small oval window as the sun began to rise on the horizon.

I caught sight of a house in the distance, not dissimilar to the one I had left back in the US. I wanted it to burn to the ground until nothing but a pile of ash was left where it had once stood. I wanted Adam and Stephanie to be inside, to feel the flames lick their skin, to inflict intense physical pain upon them both. *It still would not match the suffering they inflicted upon me.*

The family behind me stirred me from my revenge-driven reverie, as they scrambled to get order amongst them. The youngest child, no older than three or four, all blonde curls and blue eyes, wailed because the iPad had been taken from them. I winced. Their cry tugged at my heartstrings. *I will never know what it is like to be a mother.*

I watched as the family disembarked from the plane, grateful that no children had been caught up in this mess, in Adam's betrayal. No child deserved to be brought up in a broken home.

Perhaps my body's inability to produce a child should have been seen as a silver lining to this ominous cloud of hurt I was shrouded in, but I could not see beyond my self-loathing, beyond my melancholy and my failures - both as a partner and of a woman. *If I had provided Adam with the family, he so desired, would he have still sought comfort in my best friend?*

Five

Nico

Amid the shimmering azure waves and the gentle rustle of palm trees, the white sandy beach lay deserted; not a single sandcastle remained. I inhaled deeply, the scent of saltwater mingled with the sweet fragrance of sunscreen filled my lungs.

Today Aphrodite's was swarmed with families; a bitter reminder of something I no longer had. Each one hoping to find solace in the cool embrace of the indoor restaurant, sipping on ice-cold drinks and eating ice-creams. *Today is going to be a highly profitable day*, I thought as I glanced at them all from behind the bar, trying to avoid interacting with them as the pain of my loss was still raw even all these years later. Today was the anniversary of their deaths and this morning had been a struggle to emerge from my cocoon of misery. I was only here because Andreas had all but dragged me out of my apartment this morning.

He knew how difficult it was for me, but he also knew that the distraction of work would be more beneficial than wallowing in self-pity. "Nico..." he sighed, as he patted me on the shoulder. "I can manage if you want to go home." I shook my head as I watched the servers, taking orders and retrieving drinks.

Keeping this restaurant profitable in such a stale economic state had become my life's ambition. I refused to let my father down. He had founded Aphrodite's and had built its reputation to the glowing five-star recommendations on TripAdvisor. His words of wisdom echoed in my mind. *"Today may be a good day, but tomorrow is never guaranteed."*

I had watched as various restaurants in this area had dramatically declined in the past few years. The threat of another financial depression across Europe and the impending cost-of-living crisis had affected communities and businesses that relied heavily on tourism. *Businesses like mine.* Failure was not an option, even if I had to slog my guts out to make it work, I would *never* sell Aphrodite's.

All my life I had helped serve here. As a small boy, no older than ten, Andreas and my father taught me how to make myself useful around the place; from cutting up fresh ingredients before going to school to clearing tables and washing plates when I had returned. It was relentless and grueling, especially when I was at college. I tried to juggle my studies around the hours I put into the restaurant which not only affected my grades, but also my social life.

At the time I resented that childhood, the arduous upbringing of the family-run business, sacrificing the parties with friends for washing plates with two stubborn old men for company, but now I appreciated their efforts, I had the knowledge to run this place. Besides this was where Lara and I became close, hired as a waitress, we spent a lot of time together. We would walk to Aphrodite's from college and throughout our shifts we talked and joked. It was Lara who made those tiring hours more enjoyable.

It was also here Lara and I shared our first shy kiss and an awkward fumble of two teens who had no idea what they were doing.

Needless to say, our blossoming romance had become well known in the local community as things got serious, throwing a huge party for our rushed marriage before it became public knowledge that Lara was pregnant with Eve.

So, it was only natural that their tragic deaths had hit the community hard. Their pitiful looks and melancholy comments only added to my suffering. I had to disappear for a while, I had tried to run from the memories that lurked within these walls, but hiding in my apartment was no better. Waiting for the sweet embrace of death to take me to them both, allowing my misery to consume and torture me.

Andreas, the gentle giant of the coast, a war veteran and loyal friend of my father, had been my guiding light; not only for keeping the business afloat, but to navigate the murky depths of the melancholy I was drowning in. I owed him my life. Without him, I would not be here now.

"Nico, we must talk," he sighed, clutching at my shirt and pulling me into the small office behind the bar. The guests slowly petered out as the lull of the afternoon crept in; the coolest part of the day when tourists and locals would enjoy the sunshine without the threat of burning under the tropical rays.

"Nico, I am really worried about you," he said once the door had been shut behind us. I tried not to roll my eyes, instead my eyes scanned the room, making mental notes of what else I could do over the winter months to renovate the place. *First, I will remove this ghastly wallpaper and declutter all those shelves.*

I respected Andreas like an uncle. From a young age, I had listened to his words of wisdom and learned a lot about the running of the business from him. As my father's best friend, they had originally bought Aphrodite's together, with Andreas as a silent partner. Together they had made it the success that it was today; until the day came when my father could buy out Andreas' share. Yet even when Andreas had no ties to the business, he had remained loyal working in the kitchen as he had always loved, stepping up to help manage the place following my father's fatal heart attack.

In reality, he was in no fit state to still be working - arthritis in his joints and a long line of various illnesses. I felt awful that he had put off his retirement to help me. These long shifts stood on his feet and the back-breaking tasks he carried out played havoc on his joints, but not once did I ever hear him complain. I respected his professional advice, yet I was tired of this repetitive conversation about my personal life. "You need to live, Nico. You need to find joy and happiness in your life."

I had joy and happiness with Lara and Eve, but they had been cruelly snatched from me. Their faces flashed before me, beaming smiles greeting me after a long grueling day. I shook my head to clear them, but Andreas saw it as a response to his words.

"*Agori mou*, my boy, I know you have suffered, more than I can ever imagine, but you are still too young to be miserable for the rest of your life." His sigh rattled in his chest, a bout of hacking coughs ensued, making the bottle of water tremble in his hands. "Your father would not want you to follow him so soon, and definitely not before me."

His eyes pierced my soul, a subtle hint to the thoughts that had frequented my mind following the incident. My wish was to be among them, to be reunited with Lara and Eve once more. I remembered the times I had walked out into the sea, straying out into treacherous depths of the coast. I had wished for the tide to take me to them; to take me to their watery graves so I could find peace.

Each time an unseen force would drag me back to the beach, indicating that it was not yet my time to depart from this world, but each time my heart would harden further, until it was as solid as stone surrounded by impenetrable walls.

Andreas understood the loss I had suffered more than anyone else. His pain was etched in the deep grooves and wrinkles on his face. Deep furrows along his brow, his frown lines were more profound than the creases by his eyes when he smiled. He understood my constant torment of being unable to prevent their deaths. His first wife Margretta died in childbirth, but decades later he had moved on and is still happily remarried to his second wife, Maud. Though he never had any children of his own, he had treated me as his son, trying to encourage me to move on and find happiness the second time around as he had. *But that will never happen, I had my one shot of love and happiness, there will never be anyone who could replace all I have lost.*

"It's natural to long for what is gone, Nico, but it is time you find something you are willing to fight to stay alive for." His eyes scanned the still and calm restaurant through the small window in the door. "This place will still be standing, it will still turn a profit, Nico, but your life will slip you by." His hand rested on my shoulder, he squeezed it as he spoke. "Before you know it, Nico, you will be an old man like me, and instead of a life full of love and happiness, you will have one full of nothing but regrets."

The moon rose in the velvet night sky, illuminating the tranquil expanse of the calm ocean. It cast a silvery glow upon the gentle ripples of the waves. It was a clear night, the twinkling stars clearly visible from my stance below as I stood at the water's edge. The warmth of the sea lapped at my bare feet. I wriggled my toes as the gritty sand squished between them.

I heard them whisper my name in the ocean breeze earlier that afternoon, but I had been too busy to heed to their calls. Only when the restaurant was closed for the night could I go to them. Andreas' words echoed in my mind. *"It is time you find something you are willing to fight to stay alive for... instead of a life full of love and happiness, you will have one full of regrets."*

Andreas had been able to move on and let his ghosts rest, but I could not do the same. I was not ready to let them go, not able to face the finality of their demise no matter how many years had passed. *I cannot lose them forever.*

I miss you Lara, I thought, my eyes cast towards the horizon where the darkness of the sea met the sky. I felt my daughter's annoyance at being left out, I visioned her pouting lips and sulky face. She may have only been four when she died, but in death as well as in life she made sure her presence was known. *Don't worry, I miss you too, daddy's little angel.*

A symphony of cicadas provided a soothing backdrop to the whispered conversations I had with the ghosts of my past, the one-sided conversations I held with them most nights. Tonight however, a figure in the distance caught my eye. A ray of sunshine amid the lingering blanket of darkness.

Illuminated only by the faint glow of the streetlight above her. Long tumbling dark hair fell past her large breasts, a stark contrast against the sunshine yellow dress that floated elegantly in the wind. She was elegant and poised; she had come here alone.

I watched her from the shoreline, knowing I had never seen her here before, yet it was clear when Andreas embraced her that he knew who she was. I slowly approached, dragging my feet in the sand to slow my strides as I neared, catching snippets of their conversation. The bulge inside my shorts started to throb at the sight of her, seeing her full plump lips shine as her lip-gloss reflected the streetlight. Instantly I visioned them around my cock, the irresistible feeling of them flitting against the base and devouring my balls.

"nai, echo erthei monos einai mia makra istoria" She said in fluent Greek. *Yeah, I have come alone. It's a long story.*

'How did you know where to find me?" Andreas asked.

"I came here because I remembered you used to work here. Though I didn't expect you still would be Uncle -"

"Uncle?" I muttered under my breath, stopping in my tracks. I swerved out of sight hiding behind the stack of parasols so that neither of them would notice me as I eavesdropped.

"I am here for a week or so..." she said, her voice cracked.

"Come stay with me, come meet my wife," Andreas suggested.

"Thank you, but I am tired," she declined, "it has been a long day and I am staying in the villa not far from here... *Demeter Villa*"

A brief silence ensued between them, I knew of that villa, I had been there a few times. It was a popular place for honeymooners on the island or hen parties. A smirk crept on my face as I imagined her petite body splayed on the king-size bed inside; it was too large not to share it with someone. *I will happily keep her company.*

"Come back tomorrow, it has been such a long time and I have missed you, Cali." Andreas said, snapping my attention away from the naked images of her. I chanced a peak at her once more, witnessing her place a delicate kiss on his cheek, hoping she was not always so coy.

"Of course," she said, giving him a light smile before walking off into the distance, her hair fanning behind her as she passed unaware of my presence. I inhaled the fragrance that followed her; a delicate balance of floral notes. That smell was hypnotic and lingered for several moments in her wake.

My cock pressed against my zipper. I had not even gotten a proper look at her and my body was reacting to her as if I was a horny teenager. I knew I should forget about her, that I should honor the respect I had for Andreas, but I could not deny my want for her. *I do not care if she is Andreas' niece, I am going to fuck her and she is going to beg me for more.*

"Nico, you can come out now." Andreas' voice called. I skulked out of the shadows to face him. "That was my niece, Cali, you don't mind if she hangs around here? If I had known she was coming I would have taken some time off."

I shook my head, I knew I should have offered him a few days away from the restaurant, to reconcile with his niece, but my own selfish thoughts had occupied my mind. "Not at all Andreas, she is your family."

"As are you, Nico." Andreas replied. His eyes pierced mine as he gave me a silent warning - stay away from Cali.

Yet it was her who I thought of when I returned to my apartment, her name rolling off my tongue as I thrashed my cock with my eager need of release. My fist gripping tightly to my shaft as I stroked its length with no abandon, imagining it was her tight slit. Envisioning her perfect hourglass figure before me, running my hands over her full breasts cupping them as I brought them to my lips. I wanted to feel those ass cheeks spill into the palms of my hands as I gripped them tightly; to see it wobble as I smacked it so hard it left red handprints over the surface of each one.

The urge to see those plump lips devour my cock as I fucked her face, to see her eyes water as she stared up at me from her knees, watching her swallow every drop of my hot cum as it cascaded down her throat.

I suddenly erupted like a volcano at the thought of her sucking it dry. The thick white ropes sprayed high in the air, as the purple engorged tip jerked forcefully with each jet. It coated my finger and knuckles while I fantasized about it covering her gorgeous naked body.

Fuck. A wave of guilt gripped me, feeling the ghost of Lara watching from the shadows as the realization hit me; Cali was the first woman I had ever fantasized about following Lara's death.

Six

Cali *- yesterday.*

The Grecian sun pounded against my skin from the moment I stepped off the plane. Sweat trickled down my spine, and my stonewashed jeans clung uncomfortably to my legs. Even fanning myself with the free brochures hadn't cooled me down. *I will buy the first dress I see,* I told myself as I approached the queue for Passport Control. I glanced down at my passport and chose the shortest queue. Greek Nationals.

"Calista Elliana Papadopoulos" the officer read aloud "Welcome home" he said with a smile. Home. This small paradisiacal island had not been my home since I was a child. I could not remember the last time my feet touched Greek soil. My eyes scanned across the bustling Diagoras airport. Long queues of tourists snaked through the chicane barriers. *My nationality has served me well, for once.* The Ellinikí Astynomía, the Hellenic Police, took their time rigorously checking their travel documents, none of them receiving the same warm greeting as me.

I grabbed my cherished passport and tucked it away in my handbag before darting over to the Hellenic duty-free shops. A smile crept onto my face as I remembered a debate from my teenage years with my parents. They were always adamant about making the tedious journey to the Greek Embassy to renew my passport, and it felt like such a drag every time.

"You are entitled to both, asteraki mou, so you are keeping both," my mother had insisted. My mother was Greek through-and-through, it was at her insistence that I learnt the language, despite hardly visiting the country. My heart fluttered at the recollection of her nickname for me since I was a child - *asteraki mou*, my little star. It had been years since I had heard her say it.

"Yes, pookie, you may need it later in life." My father, a former lieutenant for the US Army, said in a voice that seemed too soft for a regimented soldier. While he was trained to be strict, he balanced his discipline with fairness and love when it came to being a father. The biggest change was when he was around my mother, he transformed into a different man—utterly devoted and soft as shit. He would have done anything for her, kissed her feet if she asked him to, everything in his power to ensure her continued happiness.

I longed for his warm brown eyes and the calming sound of his voice. He would have had the perfect words to ease my pain from this whole mess with Adam. Yet, if he were still here, I doubted Adam would have dared to make such a foolish mistake with a lieutenant's daughter. My lips curled into a smile, *not if he wanted to live.*

As I wandered through the shop, the story of how my parents met played out in my mind. It was a genuine fairytale romance. Love had struck them at first glance, accompanied by the smooth sounds of jazz in the bar where my mother worked. My father had stopped by on his last day of respite from his duties in Athens, where he was set to depart at dawn. He kept ordering glasses of cola just to steal a few moments with her, watching her every move and doing all he could to keep her engaged in conversation. I knew their story as intimately as my own. They began dating right away; my mom fell for his good looks and charm. They had instant chemistry and in less than a year, they were married. My mom had uprooted her whole life to follow my father on his military travels, and when my mother found out she was expecting me, he made arrangements to retire and for them to both settle in the US.

They were an incredible duo, a couple that was admired by all - loyal, honest and loving. I had always wished that my relationship with Adam would mirror theirs, but it was clear that Adam was not like my father. Our relationship would never be like theirs, but I was infatuated with Adam, hooked onto the small snippets of emotions he fed me, clinging onto his every word when he professed his love for me.

The passing of my father last year had taken a toll on my mother's health. Deep down, I knew she would soon join her cherished partner in the afterlife soon. I thought that if I could reconnect her with her long-estranged brother, Andreas, it would make her happy. Often, she spoke of him in her sleep, mumblings of their past and one-way conversations as she dreamed. I was hoping I could convince him to visit her before it was too late.

It was during these dark thoughts that I wandered aimlessly through the duty-free shops, picking up some essentials when I noticed this small ray of sunshine in my peripheral vision. A knee-length floaty dress made of the lightest, softest fabric in a lazy sunshine yellow. I envisioned how elegant it would look on me, how it would hug my figure. I *had* to buy it, especially with my stiff jeans chafing and irritating my skin.

When I packed up my belongings my swimsuits and summer attire was not my top priority, so I picked up a few other items as I made my way to the checkout.

I was supposed to be in Rhodes for three weeks, though I doubted I would stay for the full duration. I doubted I could stay away from my mother for that long, but I was in no hurry to tell her about Adam and his affair with Stephanie. I could not stomach telling her that she was right; that Adam had tore my heart into a million pieces as she had always predicted. Despite my excuses to rekindle a relationship between my mom and uncle, the real reason I had come was to avoid the truth; to run from the hurt Adam and Stephanie had caused.

Outside, a lineup of private taxis and their drivers awaited passengers. I scanned the signs until one caught my attention vividly – Mr. and Mrs. Roberts. A sudden jolt disrupted my stride as I moved past. Opting out of the pre-arranged, paid-for transfer meant spending forty euros on a taxi ride, yet I hated the thought of being pitied. Furthermore, I was determined not to justify why my deceitful and unfaithful ex-fiancé wasn't by my side, especially to a stranger. *Absolutely not.* As far as anyone here is concerned, I am simply a visitor here to check on my family and alert them about my mother's declining health.

As the taxi rolled along, within ten minutes of our forty-five-minute ride, I felt my eyelids grow heavy. "Rest easy, miss; I'll make sure to wake you when we get there," the driver said softly, his English hindered by his strong Greek accent.

I managed a slight, nervous smile, fully aware from numerous crime stories that falling asleep in a stranger's car was a risky move. "Sas eucharist, *thank you.*" I responded politely, trying to maintain a sense of calm despite my unease.

Throughout the ride to Kolympia, I was silent. I stared out at the scenery beyond the window, the built-up areas of tall buildings and houses, shops and restaurants dwindling into nothing but vast empty fields of green.

For miles, the only signs of life were small pop-up market stalls set on the side of the road where locals sold their wares: anything from small trinket boxes and bracelets to large watermelons.

As we stopped in traffic, I watched in fascination as one buyer loaded these large fruits into the back of a small cart attached to his bicycle. His face scrunched with exertion as he tried to pedal away with them. As our taxi moved on, buildings began to creep back into the picture, tarnishing the beautiful countryside views into those of concrete monstrosities. Tall, modern, apartment blocks and hotels with large pools encroach on the natural landscapes.

We were not in the busy tourist spot of Faliraki, but it might as well have been. Loud pumping music boomed from bars, the streets were alive and vibrant. The place thrummed with people, laughing and chatting joyously as they strolled along the streets or sat in the open-air restaurants.

I looked at the villa description: quiet, serene views, a blissful atmosphere and a harmonious balance with nature. I gazed back outside the window; it did not fit this description. *"Excuse me, how much further?"* I asked, my voice reflecting the anxiety that flooded my mind.

He held up his hand, his smile creased the corner of his eyes. "Don't worry, miss... not long now." When he finally pulled up outside the villa, my jaw dropped. *This cannot be happening.*

Outside the building made up of natural stones and large glass panels, a huge banner welcoming the happy couple assaulted my eyes. Red rose petals lined the path past the private pool and barbeque area and into the modern, simplistic interior. Straight through to the bedroom. Our names had been intricately displayed inside a heart made out of the remaining petals. *Adam & Cali.*

His name blurred as my tears fell. I swiped at the petals angrily, allowing my anger to erupt as I brought down my fists on the soft bedding and animalistic screams escaped me until I no longer had any energy left to exert. I slumped down on the soft mattress, biting down on my lip until I drew blood, feeling the anger still simmer away in my veins like molten lava.

Suddenly there was a knock on the door. I quickly tried to compose myself, wiping away my tears and the snot that streamed from my nose with the back of my hand as I approached. A young girl stood before me, wearing the easily recognizable colors from the travel company we had booked the trip through, the name 'Adonis' written on her name tag. Her smile instantly dropped the moment her eyes landed on my tear-stained face. "Um...welcome Mrs., um-" she stopped abruptly, her face a puzzle of confusion.

"Miss Calista Elliana Papadopoulos." I said coolly, trying not to break out into sobs. "There was a change of plans."

"Oh, I see," she shifted uncomfortably as she looked at the clipboard in her hands, chewing on the pen that she held in her other hand. "Um ...I see that there have been some couple retreats and joint packages that were booked..." I grimaced, I had forgotten all about them. "Do you, um... still want to go on them as a single?" she asked, her voice betraying her awkwardness.

I shook my head, *absolutely not.* "No thank you. Please have all of this removed. I am here to see family, so I will not have time for anything that was planned." Adonis nodded her head, scribbling frantically on the clipboard.

"There *is* a spa retreat that was part of the package deal, perhaps you could still make use of that," she empathized, giving me an apologetic smile. I shrugged, all I wanted was for her to leave. She handed me the leaflet, with the details and booking date for the spa treatment before turning on her heel. Her heels clacked against the tiled floor as she scarpered.

Emotion bubbled up inside me as I sank into the soft, now petal-free bed in the master suite. This could have been the ideal honeymoon retreat. It was private and secluded, a perfect setting for savoring the intimacy of our new life together. I imagined Adam and I joyfully rolling around in these sheets. The thought made my stomach churn.

I peeled off my jeans and t-shirt, heading for the shower. Afterward, I donned the cheerful yellow dress and slipped on a pair of new sandals. I scrutinized my reflection, noticing the weariness in my eyes from the trip. I had hoped this dress would lighten my mood, but instead it only emphasized the ominous dark cloud that lingered over my head. With a sigh, I remembered a place where the food was once delightful, traditional Greek cuisine, along the coast. My stomach growled, reminding me that I had not been eating properly in these recent months; a few bites of a sandwich in the car on the way to visit my mom had become the standard.

I remembered the restaurant from my past, a place where my mother had taken me to meet my uncle while he worked. There was no way he would still work there now, but someone there might know where he lives. *Two birds, one stone.*

Seven

Nico

Under the disguise of darkness, I allowed the unfiltered thoughts of Andreas' niece to fill my head, recalling the smell of her floral fragrance once more. My cock rose in anticipation of meeting her officially in a few hours. I was not sure how I could disguise my need or want for her when I was around Andreas. I had barely laid eyes on his niece, yet here I was thrashing my shaft to my unsolicited thoughts of her for the second time in one night.

The hunger to ravish her body with my tongue, to bury my face between her thighs and devouring that sweet pussy she was hiding. I wanted to fuck her senseless, to feel my balls explode as I drove myself in her ass. I imagined what it would look like, to see her coated in my cum; to see the thick rivulets trickle down her thighs as it seeped out of her gaped ass.

My grip tightened and I stroked its length with no abandon, wishing it was her tight slit that enveloped it instead of my hand. I roared into the darkness as I came once more despite having very little left in my balls; the orgasm was furious as it gripped my chest leaving me breathless and exhausted.

Perhaps it was because she was Andreas' niece, knowing that I should respect him by taking heed of his subtle warning made me want her more, but I was not going to be cockblocked by the old man. As my ragged breaths eased, I watched as sunlight began to filter into the room, my determination rising with it. Today I will meet Cali - I will make her want me as much as I want her.

Under the hazy Grecian sun in the early hours of the morning, I went about my monotonous routine of setting out the sunbeds, the fantasy of her body still lingered in my thoughts. Suckling on her perky breasts, teasing her nipples into hard peaks until she begged for more. I smirked at the idea of her purring in her fluent Greek tongue as I thrust deep into her, and at the thought of her calling my name over and over.

"Nico!" His abrupt tone startled me. I spun on my heel to face him, my hands instinctively covering the bulge in my shorts. "I want you to meet my niece." he said, his eyes scanning my face as my eyes widened in surprise. He chuckled, patting me on the shoulder. "She will be having breakfast with us before we open. It's taken her fifteen years to return to the island... so please, for my sake, be nice."

I shrugged, trying to be nonchalant. Not trusting my voice as I nodded, grateful that my erection had now subsided in the old man's company. I grabbed the nearest sunbed and extended the legs, before throwing the plastic-covered cushion pad on top. The sound of plastic slapping against plastic reminded me of the sound of two bodies colliding. Skin against skin. *Her against me.* I felt a tingle run down my spine and my hands ball into tight fists, focusing on the pain as my nails dug into my palm instead of my ongoing fantasy. "Why is she here?" I asked, "she hasn't visited you in almost a decade."

His face fell as he slumped down onto the sunbed, muttering under his breath. "Nico, my sister and I… she disgraced the family by marrying an American soldier… I did not agree with how readily she was to ditch her culture and move around the globe with him." His hands were animated, moving frantically as he spoke, before resting his head in his hands. "Over the years, I found it hard to bite my tongue, to see how different she was…" His eyes dropped to the floor. "The last time either of them visited, I said some things I am not proud of. I am surprised that Cali even came at all."

I placed my hand on his shoulder. "It is never too late to make it right, Andreas." I soothed as I spotted a single tear roll down his cheek before he swiped it away.

"My sister, Loretta, is very sick… I fear it is already too late."

Silence ensued before a round of coughs violently shook his body. Gasping for breath he dropped to the nearest sunbed. "I am supposed to show her around, but I am in no fit state… I do not want to alarm her with my own health issues…"

The idea of being along with Cali filled me with excitement, my words tumbling out of my mouth before I could really think about the consequences. "I can do it."

His eyes shot up at mine, nodding slowly in agreement despite the reluctant look in his eyes. "Nico, she has a fiancé," he added. "Please do not complicate her life any more than it already is."

My knuckles whitened at the thought of someone else touching her; the raging jealousy of another man claiming her darkened my mood. I was not used to this possessive need for a woman, especially one I had not properly met.

I pursed my lips as his distasteful look burned through me. It was almost as if he could read my thoughts - the aching of my cock to ignite a fire within her and tempt her into adultery.

"I mean it Nico. There are hundreds of women who want you on this island; you will not drag my niece into your bullshit."

I wanted to see if Cali had a dark side, to see if I could tempt her. "Why did her fiancé not come with her then?" I asked suspiciously, though he had no time to answer. Almost on cue, her figure came into focus, wearing a white, soft linen blouse and tan shorts that barely covered her ass. Her hair was pulled into a bun but dark tendrils escaped as she walked towards us. *Fuck, she is hot.*

Her brown eyes twinkled as she smiled at Andreas, opening her arms wide ready to embrace him. "Good Morning uncle." she smiled, her eyes glancing at me briefly. Her smile faltered momentarily. "Oh…" she said, quickly straightening up and smiling anxiously at me.

"Nico, this is Cali, Cali this is Nico… the owner of this place." I offered her my hand, instead she wrapped her arms around me, embracing me as she had known me all of her life. I tried to think back to fifteen years ago, trying to envision her younger self, I felt my body stiffen.

"You don't remember me, do you?" she smiled sheepishly as she pulled away.

I could not move, my eyes following her like a hawk, every part of me felt like a predator. I struggled to envision this sexy woman as the chubby-faced thirteen-year-old who used to hang around the place - who Lara and I would occasionally babysit for some extra cash while they were here on vacation.

I knew it was wrong to want the woman who I used to look after when she was younger, but I felt my shaft stir. "Thea?" I whispered, it meant *most beautiful* in Greek, recalling how her parents would call her that rather than her actual name. It suited her more now than it did back then. "You look... *different.*"

Andreas chuckled as he brought out plates of scrambled eggs and bacon, placing Cali's down in front of her first. "Do you remember her now Nico?" He asked, a smirk plastered on his face. It was almost as if he knew that remembering her as a child would deter my unadulterated thoughts of her.

"I used to love coming here," she said, her eyes sweeping around the restaurant. "Everything looks the same." her eyes dropped to her plate before looking back at me. "Whatever happened between you and that girl...Laura, no Lorna... was it Lauren?" she asked, sipping at her freshly squeezed orange juice. "You guys were all over each other last time I was here."

"Lara." I muttered, my tone sharper than I had intended. "She *was* my wife."

A silence fell across the table, only the scraping of metal against porcelain could be heard as we ate. I avoided eye contact, tried not to be involved in their reminiscent conversation.

All day, I tried to avoid them both, keeping myself busy with various tasks around the restaurant, yet I never let her out of my sight. Admiring her as she tanned herself on a sunbed, one I had a perfect view of from the bar. Safe enough from this distance to not draw attention to myself as my mind churned out mental images of fucking her in every position known to man.

"Nico." She gasped, reaching for my hand. I had been so lost in my thoughts I had not noticed her approach the bar. Startled, I looked up at her, my eyes devouring the sight of her in the scarlet bikini she donned. I was like a deer caught in headlights, as her chocolate brown eyes bore into mine. Forcing my eyes to look up from her half-naked body glistening in sweat to her face, noticing the shadow from her oversized straw hat partially obscured one side but did not disguise her studious gaze. "Andreas told me, um..."

Her touch brought about a tingling sensation that thrummed beneath her touch; distracting me from her words. "Andreas said, um... you would show me around... a little later." A smile pulled at the corners of her lips and her cheeks blushed a faint crimson. She was nervous to be alone with me. I could see Andreas watching us from a distance, his arms folded across his chest.

I nodded, leaning closer to her. "I know just the spot too...that every woman loves the most." I winked, seeing her cheeks instantly blush. She definitely got the hint; *the sweet spot, an inch of two just inside that sweet pussy.* I smirked, enjoying her squirm a little in her seat as the crimson deepened in her face. I could feel excitement stir within her, her obvious attraction to me as her body seemed to thrum, accepting my closeness without even the faintest flicker of wanting to push me away. There was something else about her - a darkness inside that clouded her doe-like eyes, she was hurting too.

I still felt her touch linger on my skin long after Cali had returned to her sunbed. No matter how hard I tried to ignore it I could feel Andreas' glare, scolding me silently as my attention remained fixed solely on her.

The mid-afternoon sun cast Cali's shadow in front of us, attracting my eyes to its voluptuous shape as we walked side by side through the old town. There was an uneasy silence between us initially, but that evaporated the moment we stepped into the old town. The charm of this place with its old terraced buildings and cobblestone paths had embraced her, freeing her from the silence that had held her tongue.

"I had forgotten how beautiful this place was," she murmured as we strolled through the winding streets of market vendors and restaurants. "I used to love coming here and imagining what these ruins looked like back in the day." There was a twinkle in her eye as she reminisced, a genuine smile spread across those plump lips.

She ran ahead, climbing the stone steps to look out over the top of the wall. I could not help but stare at her ass, imagining all the things I would love to do to it as well as admire her sleek, toned legs; envisioning them wrapped around my waist or splayed wide before me. My eyes wandered over the curves of her body; my rigid cock rendered my legs incapable of moving. Awestruck at how she seemed to possess everything I desired of a woman.

"Nico, aren't you coming?" She called back, turning her head in my direction.

Not yet I'm not, I thought as I jogged up the steps to meet her without breaking a sweat. Her eyes widened in surprise. *I may be older than her, but I have the stamina of a man half my age.* She took a few steps, almost stumbling, reaching out for the stone wall to steady herself as she peered over it.

"How old are you Nico?" She asked, as her eyes scanned the scenery.

"Old." I responded, my body inching closer to hers, my lips against her ear. "Old enough to know better, but young enough to not give a fuck."

"You really aren't old." she smiled, suddenly turning around to face me, her breasts now touching my chest. I knew she felt my erection dig into her flesh as she did so. I leaned even closer, until our noses were almost touching. I could sense her nervousness, but her body seemed to welcome me, allowing me to invade her personal space. Her long eyelashes fluttered as she stared into my eyes. "What else did you want to show me?" she asked.

Every image of my fantasy flashed through my mind as my lips grazed against hers, when suddenly the horn of the ferry blasted behind her. Flashbacks of the incident jolted me away from her, Lara's face flashed before my eyes. "We better head back, Cali," I muttered, turning away from her. "I'm sure your fiancé would not approve of you spending too much time with me..."

Her hands gripped my wrists, stopping me from descending the stone steps. "I don't have a fiancé. He cheated on me." I stopped in my tracks and turned back to face her. "I can do whatever the fuck I want." Her eyes flickered in defiance; her full lips slightly parted as she gave me a small smile.

Our lips crashed against each other with a passion that burned deeply within. My hands gripped her hips, pressing them against my throbbing cock while her hands wrapped around my neck. The rest of the world seemed to fade into nothingness as a small flicker of happiness swelled in my chest

Back at Aphrodite's, she pulled up a chair in front of the bar, easily pretending nothing had happened between us, that our kiss had not ignited an inferno of desire within her - engulfing her every thought as she conversed with Andreas. *How could she hide it so easily?* All I could think about was how much I wanted her, how tonight I was going to break all of my rules just so I could have her every night until she goes back home. Every minute she sat before me, fully clothed and discussing the mundane stuff was a waste.

Her eyes caught mine during a pause in her conversation, there was a twinkle in them that I knew well as she sipped her drink through the pink plastic straw. I watched as her cheeks hollowed, how her delicate throat moved when she swallowed as she maintained eye contact with me.

"Nico?" Andreas' voice snapped me out of my trance, his brow furrowed. I apologized, shaking the thoughts of her lips wrapped around my cock from my mind. "I asked if you wanted to join us for dinner this evening at my place? Celine is cooking your favorite."

I turned away to find something to keep me busy as disappointment filled me, I wanted Cali's undivided attention, not to be some sort of fucking third wheel at a family reunion. "I'll pass this time..."

"Aw I'd love it if you came, Nico." Cali's voice chimed, her words fluttered in my chest. I squashed them down, shaking my head. "There is some stuff I need to do here." I looked at her again, she was leaning forward in her chair, the top buttons of her blouse still undone from our brief fumble. She squeezed her arms together, plumping her breasts even more. A subtle gesture that went unnoticed by Andreas, but not by me. My concentration on the glass in my hand faltered and it fell from my hand, shattering instantly as it hit the tiled floor.

"Shit." I cussed while a small chuckle escaped her lips. "Andreas... could I get something to eat? All that walking has given me an appetite." Her eyes flickered in my direction briefly followed by a small polite smile. Andreas nodded, slowly rising from his chair, giving me a suspicious look before disappearing into the kitchen.

There was an awkward silence, I could feel my desire for her rampaging through my veins like a wild bull. Frustrated I snatched up the broom and pan from the far end of the bar; feeling her eyes watching my every move. It took all of my self-restraint to carry on and sweep up the broken glass. I refused to yield to her burning gaze, keeping my back to her in my vain attempt at calming down the boner that throbbed in my pants. Meticulously I swept, trying to ignore her - only once all of the shards had been cleared away did, I look back at her.

Those dark brown eyes had me hooked, I couldn't wait to fuck her, to stare into those eyes as I thrust deep and hard into her tight, neglected pussy. Cali seemed to ignite a fierce, primal urge within me that I had never experienced before, not even with Lara. Our attraction had been a slow-burn, friends to lovers, this attraction to Cali, it was something else entirely. *I have to fuck her.*

My cock hardened in my pants, watching her slide seamlessly out of her seat and saunter around the bar closer to me. "Is there anything I can help with?" she asked, standing too close, her thigh inches from my crotch. I ditched the cloth in my hands and pushed her against the back of the bar, hands either side of her body, pressing my bulge between her thighs. She gasped, as her body hit the shelving unit behind, causing the glass bottles of spirits to rattle.

I smirked as I ground my hips against hers. The moment our groins connected, a low growl resonated from my chest. Smelling her, being this close to her, it was dangerous. I could feel my self-control slipping. I stole a kiss, one that left her breathless. "I'm sure I can think of something."

Eight

Cali

My breath caught in my throat as my uncle's sudden reappearance caught us off guard. "Cali... a word," he muttered, ushering me into the office. I followed silently, head bowed as if I was a naughty school kid being subpoenaed to the principal's office. I sank down into one of the chairs beside the desk. A precariously stacked pile of paperwork trembled as my knee knocked against the table leg.

I knew getting involved with him was a bad idea, allowing my attraction to him to unfold. The moment I saw him earlier this morning, my childhood crush came flooding back with a vengeance, instantly transporting me back into my thirteen-year-old body buzzing with hormones and thoughts I could not control nor understand. The way his honey-gold eyes glinted in recognition after I pulled away from him, humiliated by my knee-jerk reaction to hug him as familiarly as I had with Andreas, as if it had not been fifteen years since I last saw them.

Though looking at Nico, you would not have believed so much time had passed between us; his sharp angular jaw set, dark stubble spread across it, and his honey-gold eyes smoldered. His fists clenched at his sides as Andreas called whisked me into the back room. *What am I doing?* I thought to myself, *throwing myself at him.* A married man of all people. My insides squirmed at the recollection of the wedding ring that glimmered under the Grecian sun as his hands fondled my breasts as we moved around the corner of the stone pillar out of tourists' immediate sights.

Andreas' eyes glowered at me as I skulked into the office and took a seat, my eyes avoiding his by taking in the peeling and faded decor of the office. My gaze lingered at the cluttered desk beside me where a pile of precariously stacked paperwork wobbled in the breeze caused by Andreas slamming the door behind him.

"You should know better, Cali! Acting like a whore... when you are soon to be married!" he bellowed, his face transforming from the kind and caring uncle I remembered into a fierce and hateful man. "This is the precise reason why I disagreed with your mother's decision to marry an American, to breed with him and raise you in the US. Americans have no morals. Liars and manipulators... the lot of them."

"But uncle-"

His intense glare cut me off. "Despite what your mother said otherwise, your father was no better... he promised Lorretta everything under the sun, but he gave her nothing but grief." His fist slammed down on the table, causing the paperwork to flutter to the ground.

"My father was a great man and an amazing father." I muttered trying to hold back the blinding tears that flooded my eyes. "You didn't even know him."

I watched as the deep grooves that lined Andreas' face softened as his expression changed, "Cali, I'm sorry... you are right, I did not know your father; I did not *want* to know him. I have been dealing with arrogant American pricks for most of my life to know they are all the same."

I shook my head, biting my lip. I refused to look at him, instead fixating on a small framed photograph of Nico, beside him was a blonde woman with gorgeous blue eyes and a child who was a miniature version of her. A lump formed in my throat.

"Cali…" Andreas' voice fluttered as he approached me, picking up the frame I was staring at. "Nico is not himself at the moment… he is still trying to get over the loss of them."

I frowned, "what do you mean?"

His shoulders slumped as he heaved a loud sigh. "Several years ago… his wife and his daughter both perished in a tragic accident…"

The rest of his words blurred in my mind; I was no longer listening, selfishly recalling his hands as they ran along my body. Guilt no longer wracked my body.

"But you are not the first woman he has set his sights on, Cali… Nico only wants one thing… I did not have you pegged to be a *slut* while your mom is dying alone in a foreign country."

I bit my lip so hard I tasted blood, fleeing the office as fast as my legs could carry me. I spotted Nico at the bar, talking to a woman with porcelain skin and bright blonde hair. Her fake tits pointing in his direction, his gaze fixated on them. I scorned myself at the jealousy that flared up inside me as their flirtatious conversation ensued. *Fuck them all.* I thought as I stormed through the restaurant, ignoring the allure to turn around at the sound of Nico's voice calling my name.

Nine

Nico

A smirk grew on my face the moment I noticed her eyeing up the blonde before me; that sliver of jealousy that flashed across her face. I had no interest in the blonde, all fake and plastic, especially not when someone like Cali was up for grabs. I had half expected her to storm over here, to commandeer my attention but instead she spun on her heel and left.

"So, what do you say... I'm free for the rest of the day..." the blonde purred; her fingertips brushing my arm, her pale gray eyes flickered beneath her heavy false lashes.

"Cali!" I shouted, rushing after her, ignoring the blonde completely. "Thea... wait!"

With her head bowed she pressed forward in angry determination. I felt my cock harden; *I like it when she is angry.* I watched as she walked farther into the distance, blending into the throng of people before disappearing altogether.

A shiver suddenly ran down my spine and my anger flared with me as I abruptly turned on my heel. *I am going to give Andreas a piece of my mind-*

"Nico." His voice snapped me to attention as Andreas stood before me, his face etched with sadness, regret lingering in his eyes.

I stood straighter, folding my arms and waited for his explanation. The lines on his forehead deepened as he scowled at me. My eyes diverted to the blonde who was unashamedly swirling her tongue around the rim of her Mythos beer; the top of its thick green bottle was around the same girth as an average male's cock. *But I am bigger than average.* Her eyes staring directly at me. Watching my reaction when she took several deep gulps of her beer before licking her lips. I imagined it was my seed she was cleaning from her face; envisioning the streaks of white glisten as they dribbled from the corners of her mouth.

Andreas sighed, "Nico... this is why I want you to stay away from Cali..." My eyes snapped to him; the sound of her name forced the vision of her face to flood into my mind. The sensation of her perky breasts beneath my hands as I caressed them hours before as our kiss grew wild and heated. I had broken the top buttons of her blouse in order to see them, to feel the bare skin in my palms. "All you are looking for is sex Nico... a temporary fix... a moment of pleasure so you no longer feel the pain. I get it, Nico. I do." Andreas said, pinching the bridge of his nose. "But you *will* leave my niece out of it."

Anger bristled as I pushed away from him; heading for the blonde and gripping her wrist. "Where is your hotel?"

We had barely made it into her hotel room before I tore off her clothes; hearing the fabric tear beneath my hands and her squeals of surprise made my cock jerk in anticipation. My anger at Andreas spurred me on; yanking on her hair and forcing her down to her knees.

Her blonde head bobbed up and down my shaft, red lipstick smearing as she took my length deep in her mouth, staining the base of it as she gagged. I drove my hips against her mouth; her eyes streaming as the throaty sounds hung heavy in the air. The blonde's hand disappeared between her splayed legs; three fingers already buried to their knuckles.

Dragging her to her feet, I bent her over the couch, grabbing hold of her ass in one hand as the other guided my cock to her bald pussy, groaning as I pushed it deep and feeling her juices coat my shaft. I spread her ass as wide as I can, pull my cock out of her pussy and drive it into her tight rosebud entrance. She squealed like an injured animal, as I forced the full length of it inside of her dry tight asshole. Within moments she succumbed to the sensation; her squeals now of delight and ecstasy as my fingers drove inside her slit.

I imagined Cali bent on all fours before me, taking my cock deep in her ass like this blonde. Envisioning coaxing similar moans from her; wanting to feel her cum coat my balls rather than this woman whose name I did not even care to ask for.

"Fuck" she yelped as her body trembled, her knees giving out before she crumpled under the intensity of her orgasm. My cock throbbed as I clutched a fistful of her hair, pulling her back into position.

"I am not finished with you yet." I growled, my other hand still coated with her sticky nectar wrapped around her throat, holding her as close to me as possible so I could push my cock harder and faster into her tight hole. I could feel it stretch around me, welcoming me as I fucked her through yet another of her orgasms. "You're a filthy whore, aren't you?" I hissed. Pulling on her hair until her neck looked as though it would snap.

She whimpered louder every time I thrust, taking me ever closer to the edge. "Nico... fill me with your cum." The vision of filling Cali with my load; her tight asshole and her pussy took me over the edge. My cum shooting like a rocket, red hot and forceful spilling out of her entrance around my cock. As I pulled out, more of it oozed from her gaping hole.

"Fuck" she shuddered once more, "that was fantastic." Her American drawl made my skin crawl as she reveled in her high. The woman before me laid on her back, her fingers exploring her slit before scooping out her juices and licking them off her fingers one by one. My cum pooled beneath her. "Are you in a rush to get back?" she murmured, her fingers still poised at her lips as a seductive grin crept across her face.

Fuck she was good. Writhing and moaning as if we were on set of a pornographic movie, the curves of her body tantalizing and alluring as my tongue explored her. I allowed myself to get lost in this moment as I became numb to the pain of my loss as she coaxed another orgasm from me; my load thinner and not as forceful this time around. In the hazy fog I called out her name; Cali. My eyes opened expecting to see her face looking back at me as my fingers clutched at the bedding on either side of her head as my load shot deep into her warmth.

I felt her slap vibrate through my skull as she scrambled out from beneath me, trails of our cum combined as it glistened on the inside of her thighs. "Get out," she hissed, wrapping herself in a robe that was discarded on the floor. "Get the fuck out.", I shrugged on my clothes and left without another word. *What was she expecting? I didn't even know her name.*

I walked through the corridors, slowly navigating my way out of this labyrinth, my body flooded with self-loathing as it always did after fucking someone new. And yet, this time was different; it was not the ghost of Lara that was haunting me, but the desire for Cali.

I found myself on the street outside her villa, sitting alone along a narrow coastal path. Trees and shrubs almost obscured the view of the sea to my left, without another villa for at least another mile or so along this path it was secluded and private. My breath ragged and the stench of sweat and sex on my skin. A skeletal hand clutched my wrist, instantly causing my beating heart to freeze. "Nico, don't do this." Lara's words echoed in my ears, clawing at my heart like sharp talons. I shook my head, my gaze shooting through her to the black waves of the ocean, illuminated by the soft silver glow of the full moon overhead.

Lara's pain suddenly hit me like a jab to the abdomen, knocking the air out of my lungs. Her figure began to solidify before me. Her black sunken eyes gave me a haunting stare. Her skin was pale, her once beautiful golden curls now bedraggled and sodden. *This* was not how I had wanted to remember her. In life she had been vibrant and full of smiles, but now she looked like a being from my darkest nightmares. Her skeletal limbs moved closer to me, "Nico..." her whispered voice mixing with the wind whipping through the leaves of the palm trees nearby.

I did not understand; *why is Lara interfering now?* I had been with multiple women, she had never stepped in to stop it before, only her simmering anger resonated after the deed was done. *So why now?*

"She is different..." Her voice whimpered. "I can feel it, Nico... don't open Pandora's box... I will lose you."

I opened my mouth to protest, but a flood of images made the words clog in my throat. The images of Cali; my fantasies of her; those full plump lips curling into a smile, the sound of her melodic voice. I felt the armor inside me crack, just a little. I had already broken two of my rules with her; *is this such a good idea?* I hesitated taking another step closer to the villa; *what if Lara is right? What if it's different this time? What if this is more than lust?*

Cali's cry pierced the night sky, shattering my resistance. I rushed to the villa following the sounds of her distress. Though as I stood there, my eyes absorbed the view before me as my breath fogged the glass; it was not cries of distress that escaped her. They were moans of pleasure.

Ten

Cali

My insides were on fire, my body drenched in sweat. I held no control over my actions, as my hand crept between my thighs massaging the outer walls of my slit. My fingers teasing my hungry entrance. *Nico.* I was wet just thinking of him fucking that blonde, his cock deep inside her - I wished it was me and not her.

As I replayed the scene of him touching me, his hands urgently seeking my breasts; cupping them and pinching my nipples as his tongue sought mine. I wondered what being with Nico would be like; no doubt from the brutal way he kissed that seemed to bruise my lips it would be painfully pleasurable. In my mind, I played out how I wanted the scene to end; his fingers trailing beneath my panty line; feeling his chunky fingers spread my inner folds and slip a finger inside.

My breathing became throaty groans as my fingers worked in and out of my damp core, thrusting deep inside. My clit tingled in excitement, wanting Nico's fingers to replace my own.

My fingers were not long nor wide enough to imitate his nor to hit that spot, the sweet spot my body yearned for to trigger my orgasm. I groaned; I needed to be filled, to be stretched as more of my fingers pounded away at my slit. I looked around; seeking out anything that was phallic shaped that would work. At home I had toys - lots of them. Adam had always fucked with a singular agenda, always driven with his need to cum rather than my pleasure. I needed more to reach a true climax. My toys had been carefully selected; each one stimulating a different orgasm depending on my mood. Yet here I had nothing. That was when I spotted it; the thick, smooth handle of my hair brush lying on the bedside dresser. Snatching it I wasted no time burying it inside me; tilting it slightly so that it grazed my inner walls as I rammed it hard and fast into my hungry pussy.

The squelch of my juices coating the handle filled the silence before my moans grew louder; my mind lost in the bliss of my impending release. I was a ticking time bomb, about to explode at any moment.

"Yes... fuck yes..." I screamed loudly, as I reached the precipice of my climax, my pussy swallowing the entire handle, my juices soaking the lower bristles. I wanted Nico, I wished he were fucking me and not the blonde, he had revealed his brutal nature in the way he kissed and tugged at my nipples. I wanted him to tear me apart and claim me as his own.

I pumped harder until my wrists ached, stifling my moans by biting my bottom lip. *"Are you ready?"* his voice purred in my mind as I pictured his golden caramel eyes glowering in lust. *Oh, I am ready. So ready.*

My orgasm quaked my body, my breathing ragged and uncontrollable as my free hand grabbed at my naked breast before scrunching the bedding above my head. My back arched as my orgasm rippled through my body and my core gripped the plastic intruder. Only once it had finally ebbed did I open my eyes.

My scream clogged my throat, my heart hammered against my ribs. Time froze as did the blood in my veins as two pools of molten gold penetrated mine.

"You really should lock the door."

"Nico!" I gasped, gathering the bedding around my naked torso, my insides melted and my cheeks burned in shame. His intense gaze pinned me down, his desire smoldered in his eyes. Words evaded me, my brain forgot how to work. His eyes never left mine.

The thought of him watching, his cock erect in his trousers like a steel pipe stoked the fire in my core. It throbbed uncontrollably, the hairbrush still stuffed inside it. My eyes lingered on the outline of his shaft, trying to push aside my humiliation of being caught masturbating with a hairbrush of all things. "What are you- how did you-"

Nico was not smiling. His jaw was clenched and his eyes smoldered with lust. His towering figure filled the gap where the door had once been, his scent of sandalwood and vanilla hit my nostrils, along with the unmistakable smell of sex. My insides squirmed. *He has come to take me after having her.*

I knew I should be disgusted, revolted even, the thought of being with a man who has already fucked someone and left them to come here. But the fact he was here, rigid, and ready to fuck sent my mind into a tizzy. All thoughts of safe-sex and vanilla caresses were gone in Nico's presence. I seemed to unravel before him.

He took a step closer. He exuded danger, his eyes fierce and wild like the heartless beast Andreas had portrayed him to be. Judging by the solid mass that threatened to rip through his shorts, there was no going back. He was going to devour me, tear me apart, make me beg for mercy. All the things I had fantasized about. *I was his.*

"I heard you tell Andreas where you were staying," he said, with a voice as smooth as silk. A small groan escaped his lips. He reached for the brush still clamped in my tight pussy. He eyed me quizzically as he slowly removed it, admiring the juices that glistened on it in the light. I averted my gaze, my cheeks on fire in shame.

"Did you- *with her?*" I asked breathlessly as he jammed his fingers deep into my slit. My eyes popped open, two of his fingers, using them to guide me to my feet.

"Do you want the truth?" He murmured, his breath hot against my ear as he held me close just by the two fingers buried in my core. I tentatively nodded, surprisingly aroused by the thought of him fucking another woman. "Kiss me and find out."

My lips crashed against his, tasting her on his tongue; it was wrong to feel so aroused yet so jealous. Nico smirked, his other hand threaded into my hair, allowing tendrils to slip through them before clutching a fistful and pulling.

"Was she good?" I murmured, grinding my hips against his fingers working myself up to another orgasm.

"She was not *you.*" His fingers released me and I fell to the bed. He wasted no time, spreading my legs as wide as they would go before lowering his face to my soaked entrance. "Is that what you were fantasizing about, *Thea*. Me fucking that blonde at the bar?" I groaned as his tongue curled along my folds, teasing me. "Did you wish I was here fucking you instead of a *hairbrush.*"

I groaned once more, out of embarrassment this time. Nico chuckled; I felt his lips curl into a smile before thrusting his tongue deep inside my slit. My hands automatically grabbed clumps of his hair, guiding his face deeper into my core until his nose was pressed against my clit. The warm exhalation of his breath danced over it, delicious and enchanting as his tongue pressed against the sweet spot.

I could feel myself dampening, my blush deepening on my cheeks. If he carried on like this I would explode in his mouth. I screamed his name as I bucked beneath him, grinding my hips against his face. "Nico..." I purred trying to pull his head away as the urge to clench my legs together ripped through my body.

"NO" he roared, inserting his fingers and suckling on my clit. "I want to taste you... I want you to come in my mouth." I shuddered under his tongue, encouraged by his words to let go of the pressure that had been bottled up inside me. I had opened the floodgates as wave after wave of my orgasm gripped me; my thighs clenched around his head and my hands held his face firm in position as the powerful orgasm gripped me.

When he resurfaced, my cum was dripping from his chin. It had unlocked something within him, as he tore off his clothes and launched himself on top of me like a wild animal. His mouth left wet and sloppy kisses along my collarbone, his teeth grazing the tender flesh of my neck until his lips found mine once more. Tasting myself on his tongue was even better than tasting her; it felt so taboo to enjoy the taste of my own cum.

The kiss was ferocious, all teeth and tongues as he positioned himself over me; his solid mass firmly pressed up against dripping heat. My nails clawed at his back, digging deep into his spine. I wanted him, *needed* him. I was trying to coax him into thrusting his pelvis forward, just an inch more so my slit could envelop him. "Not yet he purred." pulling away, climbing onto his knees. "There is one more place where you can still taste her." He groaned, placing the tip of his shaft against my lips.

Its head was engorged, purple and veiny, peeping through his foreskin. I had never been with someone who was uncut. The idea of the excess flesh both scared and aroused me. I watched as he drew his foreskin back, revealing the angry looking tip; his honey-gold eyes staring down at me as his thighs gripped around my neck.

The scent of sex oozed from his shaft, my lips parting instantaneously inviting it inside. He growled as he eased it in, inch by inch. The moment the tip hit the back of my throat I almost choked; I knew Nico was bigger than Adam, but my nose was still an inch or two away from the base of his shaft.

My eyes flicked up to his, seeing the glint of amusement in his eyes as he lowered the last few inches inside. I tucked away my teeth and hollowed my cheeks as he fucked my mouth as hard and as deep as he desired; my eyes filling with tears as each stab to the back of my throat made me gag, but not once did I break eye contact.

"Fuck... *Thea.*" He moaned, his shaft twitching against my tongue, hearing his groan deepen as the hot, salty taste of his cum filled my mouth. "You are such a good girl." He growled, his hand holding my head in place as I swallowed every drop of his load. I loved the taste of cum, the taste of *him*, but I was disappointed that there was very little. *He has used it all on her.* I thought as I stared into his eyes.

"I shouldn't have wasted it on *her.*" He groaned, pulling out and collapsing on the bed beside me.

My jealousy bristled; "You should have followed me, Nico... you should have had me first."

His lips silenced me, his touch gentle as his fingertips brushed tendrils of hair from my face. "I wish I had *Thea...*" He muttered, his voice distant and his eyes avoiding eye contact with me as his other hand flitted along my bare skin, twisting my nipples before crushing it in his palm. "Believe me, I wished she was you."

My body shook, a small squeal escaped me as his lips worked their way down to my erect nipples. Nipping at them and rolling them delicately between his teeth, sending ripples along my body. A low chuckle rumbled from his chest before he suddenly threw my hands up over my head, pressing them into the soft-foam mattress. "Just because I have no cum left to give does not mean I cannot fuck you senseless." He said, his eyes penetrating mine with a hunger I had never seen before.

I was caught in his possessive grasp, held in place by his firm grasp on my wrists and his engorged member as it pressed against my pelvis. His throbbing tip just below my belly button. The sensation of fireworks exploding across my skin as he alternated between gentle, playful nibbles and furious, soul-destroying kisses as he slid his member inside my warmth.

"I should punish you," he growled, tugging at a nipple with his teeth. "For walking away from me." His hips drove in a slow deep rhythm, only allowing the tip of his cock to enter. "I should tease you... make you beg to cum."

My murmured response inaudible gasps as I ground my hip against his tip. "Or are you going to be a good girl and do as I say from now on?" he snarled, his breath was hot against my nipple as he spoke, slowly lifting his head to look directly into my eyes. He suddenly took me, I yelped as my walls suddenly stretched to accommodate his full length. Being so thick and big, it brushed against the spot with every thrust; I was nearing the verge of another orgasm, his lips crashing down against mine, swallowing my moans.

"*Thea,*" his purred, suddenly stopping, his voice hardening and becoming firm and authoritative, devoid of any emotion. "Turn around. Now."

I was too aroused to object, to question the sudden change in him. I wanted him. I wanted my release. I obliged, kneeling on the bed, resting on my elbows. His tip rubbed against my entrance. My inner walls stretched to accommodate him; I gasped as I felt his thighs meet mine.

"Isn't this better than your *hairbrush*?" His words came as a low growl, as he drove his cock in deep and forcefully. My body responded eagerly as his hands held my hips firmly, guiding me with each powerful thrust. His fingers dug into the flesh as he pulled apart my ass cheeks. I found myself unable to stifle the sounds of pleasure escaping my lips, whimpers and moans as I surrendered completely to the brutal rhythm he set.

Nico's brutality made Adam's touch seem dull and immature. I felt as if I had been awakened, my sexual appetite had finally met its match. I yearned for this carnal, filthy attraction. My desire to be fucked into oblivion. *Nico is mine; everything about him including his monster cock is mine.*

In an unexpected move, his hand tugged at my hair, then encircled my throat, drawing me closer to him as his primal force continued to invade my depths. "Only I have the right to your pleasure," he asserted with a deep, resonant growl. "You are mine."

"Gamóto me sklirótera...*fuck me harder.*" I cried, clutching at anything my hands could get hold of - his hair, his flesh, the bedding. "Naí! Naí!... *Yes! Yes!*"

Waves of pleasure surged through me as I sensed my peak approaching. The raw intensity of his movements, combined with the relentless force of his thrusts, sent my body into a frenzy of ecstasy.

My hands grabbed my breasts, squeezing and pinching my nipples, allowing this dark wave of lust to engulf me. The harder he thrust, the harder I pinched, until I was teetering my climax, begging to be allowed to cum.

"Please... I'm so close." I moaned, matching his rhythm, one hand now circling my clit, feeling my nectar leak from my slit. He responded, not with words, but by forcing my body back down to the bed, and buried my face deep into the bedding.

I struggled to breathe through the fabric, which only heightened the sensation of reaching the precipice of my orgasm. My body quaked violently, "Gamó...*fuck...*" I screamed over and over, spasming hard against his throbbing shaft as a furious surge flooded from my core, soaking the bedding beneath my trembling knees.

Nico was silent for a moment, his hands still gripping my ass tight, a slight tremor coursed through his fingertips. Before abruptly he let me go, I had not been expecting it. My body crumpled into a heap, quivering and shaking in the aftermath of the most intense orgasm I had ever experienced. I took several deep breaths before opening my eyes.

But he was gone. He had slipped away, silently closing the door behind him as I quivered in the aftermath of my orgasm, too preoccupied to have noticed. He disappeared like a phantom in the night. It was as if this had just been a figment of my imagination, but my cum saturated the bedding beneath me, dribbling from my satisfied slit that had been stretched and abused by him. Sitting upright, I noticed a torn piece of paper with his number left on the bedside - a prominent reminder that this had not been a dream.

My body trembled as his touch lingered on my skin. Disbelief filtered through my brain. *I fucked Nico Karamanlis; I tasted another woman's cum and I enjoyed it.* My uncle had warned me about him.

This womanizing hunk who only wanted one thing, and one thing only. Uncle had warned me not to end up in his bed. *Well, technically, he ended up in mine.* I smirked.

The room suddenly felt cold, goosebumps rising on my skin and a shiver rippled across my naked body. I cursed as I gathered up the bedding from the floor, swaddling myself in it. The musky smell of sex and cum lingered in the air, the faint hint of his cologne still tormented me. I found myself longing for his strong, muscular arms to wrap around me; to nestle in his warmth and breathe his masculine smell.

It was surprising how much you could tell about a person from the way they kissed; Nico was raw and intense, passionate and animalistic. He was everything I had never experienced before, a demanding lover - someone who took what he wanted and was selfish in his desires.

Nico was everything Adam never could be. I snuggled deeper into the duvet, my frustration bubbled inside at his sudden absence - leaving without saying a word. *Did I do something wrong?*

Eleven

Nico

I should have listened to Lara. I should have walked away and forgot Cali existed. There were always other women. But I had to have her and now there was no going back.

From my moment I laid eyes on her, sprawled on the king-size bed pumping the handle of her hairbrush into her tight slit; watching as it came out slick with her juices, I had lost all of my control. Hearing her cries of pleasure inflicted by this everyday object bristled deep within, unleashing a possessive beast I never knew existed. It claimed her; envious of something other than me bringing her pleasure.

Now as I lay in the darkness of my empty flat, my mind replayed the scene over and over, evading sleep once more. Thinking about the way her body arched as she came over my face and the way she swallowed my cock made me shudder. *Why had I wasted my time and effort on the blonde when I could have made a mess all over Cali instead?*

Rays of the early morning sun danced through the gaps in the curtains, I wondered how Cali had slept, smirking when I imagined her blissfully sleeping with a satisfied grin plastered to her face. *Why do I care? I got what I wanted.* But that was not true, as soon as our lips connected, I felt that magnetic pull, a lure that made me want more. *One night with Cali was not enough.*

I ran the shower cold, hoping the icy jets of water would numb my body, if not my mind, of Cali's touch. I tried not to think of the way she succumbed to every inch of my cock as I buried it into her mouth or the delicious way she presented her ass to me as I took her from behind. Juicy and round like an apple, tempting me to take a bite. I sighed, *one night with Cali is definitely not enough.* There was still so much I wanted to do to her - *with* her.

While wrapping the towel around my waist, I caught a glimpse of the angry red grooves Cali had carved into my flesh, reaching from the base of my neck to my waistline. I stood staring at them over my shoulder in awe, recalling that moment. Losing myself in those dark brown eyes of hers as I felt her pussy tighten around me. I had felt her nails pierce the skin; the pain had snapped me out of my trance just before I was about to kiss her again, to smother the sounds of her orgasm with my lips. I knew I was opening up to her more and more with each kiss and exposing my vulnerability.

For years I lived by those three rules; no strings, no face-to-face, no kissing. But with Cali, I had broken them all. *I will not develop feelings for Cali.* I told myself firmly, yet the thought felt like a lie. *Why had I not listened to my dead wife?*

Every minute ticked by with agonizing torture - waiting for Cali to arrive, steeling myself from the sudden flood of emotions that the thought of her evoked. I was not ready to feel them. The clock's incessant ticking echoed loudly in my mind, hearing it above the clatter of the busy restaurant before me. Cali was nowhere to be seen.

"Have you seen Cali?" Andreas asked, his voice jolting me out of my trance. I shook my head, unable to speak as a lump formed in the back of my throat. I watched as Andreas' eyes clouded over, the sparkle of hope that had been in them now snuffed out. "I really fucked up," he sighed. *You and me both*, I thought, feeling the hollow pit in my stomach growing by the minute.

Is she mad because of how I left? The urge to crawl beside her, to nestle my naked body against hers and fall asleep beside her had overwhelmed me. I thought leaving silently and without a word would have saved me from feeling something *more* for her; but I had already opened a can of worms - each one had wiggled beneath my armor, destroying it from the inside.

In the space of a single night, Cali had managed to bulldoze through the walls that had taken me years to build. My anger and loneliness without her presence near me sizzled through my veins like electricity, scorching and burning as more time passed. I had let her get underneath my skin. *Where the fuck is she?*

As the sun slowly disappeared beyond the horizon, appearing as though it was sinking into the watery depths of the ocean, I felt Lara beside me once more. Her disapproval reverberated through my body. "You should have listened to me, Nico." Her soft words were carried to my ears by the gentle sea breeze. "Now the time has come to choose... *her* or me?"

I turned to face her but her figure disappeared before my very eyes; emptiness enveloped me and there was a fire in my lungs that spread with a fierceness with every breath I took. The beast inside thrashed around like a trapped wild animal - desperate to escape its confines and to taste freedom once more. *Yearning for the taste of Cali once more.*

I thought back to the hairbrush lodged deep in her pussy, growling into the night air. *How could this woman make me jealous of a fucking inanimate object?* My feet stopped abruptly as I came to the fork in the road. If I followed the road to the left, I would find myself outside Cali's villa once more - teetering a path of the unknown, accepting these feelings that churned in my gut.

Instead, I steered myself to the right, forcing my feet to keep walking this familiar path - the one that led back to my empty apartment. The idea of Cali waiting for me, completely naked, pouting as she sulked in my absence. The aching desire to go to her so I could kiss her and devour her slender body sent a shiver along my spine. I shook my head. *I am not ready.*

Twelve

Cali

"You kept me waiting." Four little words spoken in his dulcet tones, his caramel eyes bore deep into mine as he leaned against the doorframe, looking every bit as fierce and possessive as I had recalled from the night before. My insides squirmed at the sight of him; I was unable to respond before his lips sought mine with such force that he pinned me against the wall and all thoughts of denying myself the pleasure of this man quickly abandoned.

Tearing at each other's clothes, I found myself entangled in Nico's strong possessive arms, his cock lodged deep in my aching pussy once more. I gave myself over to him - body, mind and soul. I was his to take.

"Nico... I want you to fill me with your cum." I gasped breathlessly. "I am not going to get pregnant." His eyes simmered when I murmured those words in his ear before a growl resonated from his chest. He rolled onto his back and gripped my hips tight in his hands.

My breasts bounced as I rode him, his hands held me firmly against him as he thrust his hips upwards to meet mine. The desperation to fill me with his seed was written all over his face as beads of sweat trickled along his brow. The more I stared into Nico's eyes, the more I felt something within me shift as a stronger, more confident side to me was unlocked. I ground my hips against him, feeling him shudder before his hot load invaded my core. His hands roaming across my body, before pulling me down to him, his tongue in search of mine. *Never had I ever felt sexier than I do in the arms of Nico Karamanlis.*

As I stared at him in the aftermath of our climax. I felt the thirteen-year-old girl in me grin smugly, delighted to finally be in the arms of her first crush. Back then it was a crush, envious of his girlfriend who got to kiss him and cuddle him whenever she wanted, but now, he was here with me. I wanted him to be mine, though I realized that I probably meant nothing to him - I was just another woman he used for his own desire. *Nico Karamanlis is a heartbreaker, fucking women to get over the loss of his wife.*

I did not regret fucking him, but I could not deny that there were deeper emotions stirring inside; feelings I did not want to feel for anyone. Especially not Nico - a man who my uncle had warned me about - a man unable to move on from the tragedies of his past.

But I was drawn to him instantly, just the sight of him made my knees weak and lit a fire in my core. He was so different to Adam in every way; from his looks to the brutal way in which Nico coaxed every orgasm to rip through my body relentlessly. Never had Adam been so rough, so demanding, so *possessive*. I found myself enjoying it, needing it, *wanting more.*

I knew that despite myself, I would not be satisfied with these brief encounters, that despite my uncle's warnings, I was falling hopelessly for a man who would never love me back. I snuggled into him, shutting off my thoughts trying to enjoy the warmth of his body against mine - trying to savor the moment before he disappeared again without a word.

My fingertips drew small circles on his back absentmindedly as my eyes roamed over his sleeping face. Taking in every line, every feature of his restful and expressionless face as if committing it to memory. My heart swelled as suddenly his eyes flickered open, their honey-gold piercing mine. "Cali" he murmured with a small smile, tightening his grip around my body before rolling me on top of him once more. "You are going to be the death of this old man," he chuckled lightly.

I felt the rigidness of his member pressing against me, as I ground my hips automatically against it. This man knew all the right buttons to press, to get exactly what he wanted. I gasped as I lowered myself down the full length of him; my heat now molded to fit him comfortably. Residue of his cum from earlier made it slide in easily, along with my nectar that seemed to flow from within like a tap. Soon, wet sliding sounds resonated as I worked my way up and down his length in long strokes while his lips ravished me. My nails dug into his shoulders seeing the small white crescent indentations left in his skin as I neared another climax.

I knew he was close too; his grunts and groans quietening into short shallow breaths, his hands clenched on my buttocks dragging me harder and faster along his shaft. I felt it, the moment his hot cum erupted inside me, I would *never* stop enjoying the feel of it flooding my insides.

I leaned forward and kissed him, my tongue parting his lips to deepen the kiss. He froze momentarily, before his hands surrounded my back and pulled me closer to him. The ferocity of his return took me by surprise, my orgasm quaked my body as his mouth absorbed my scream.

"Cali" he purred once more, making my skin prickle. "What the fuck are you doing to me?" he moaned.

Thirteen

Nico

I jolted awake, my body soaked in icy sweat. My heart raced wildly, and tears streamed down my face. I angrily wiped them away, repeating my father's unyielding words in an angry hiss, *"boys don't cry"*.

My eyes scanned the unfamiliar room, before lingering on her naked body beside me. I wanted to regret it. I had crossed a line, but I knew I would do it again in a heartbeat. The possessive beast inside me wanted nothing more than to ravage her at every waking moment. I had succumbed to its urges as again and again last night we fucked until our bodies could take no more. It had been more than just unadulterated lust; there was more pulling us together, strings intertwining us, as delicate and intricate like a spiderweb. *Feelings.*

My racing heart slowed the more I stared at her, knowing that for the first time in the last seven years, I did not long to see my late wife's face the moment I woke up, but Cali's.

I shook my head, trying to clear the haunting memory that tormented me each night. The nightmare that I had woken so abruptly from. It was always the same vivid images that would startle me and would crush my chest as if their loss had only just occurred.

Guilt crept over me as I acknowledged these feelings Cali stirred within me, the urge to lay back down beside her and whisper sweet nothings in her ear. Yet as the darkness started to fade, the early sun beyond the window began to rise, I knew I was already late in my duties to open up the restaurant.

I peeled the bedcovers away from my naked torso and shoved on the clothes from the night before. I did not want to leave her, but the weight of guilt that Andreas would have to set up alone otherwise dragged me away from her.

Slipping out of the villa quietly, I had not expected the heat of the morning to hit me so hard. Sweat oozed from my pores as I set a brisk pace to Aphrodite's. I felt the familiar shroud of energy surrounding me; Lara's ghostly presence joining me on my walk of shame back to Aphrodite's. The amber haze of the sun cast a singular elongated shadow before me on the street as I pressed on, trying to ignore the sizzle of her energy at my side.

My breaths hitched in my throat. The closer I walked towards the shore, the more the images from my nightmare returned and the harder it became to ignore Lara's silent triumph. Guilt gnawed at my insides. *I should have done more to stop them going, I should have protected them as I had promised I would.* I froze as I felt her arm snake though mine, her icy grip chilling me to the bone. Her voice fluttered in the sea breeze saying nothing but my name, a lament as if she knew how deep these feelings for Cali ran. I had not intended to visit her last night, I had purposely chosen the path that would lead home, yet I had still wound up at her door.

Flames engulfed everything. Thick, black smoke billowed around me. I could taste the ash lingering in the air, falling from the sky like toxic snow as the fire embraced the boat like it had been unleashed from the very depths of Hell.

I felt the cold prickle my skin as another memory overtook my nightmare. A memory I tried to bury deeper than any others. It hurt more when I remembered the good times with Lara, those snippets of time laced with happiness and hope than it did recalling the tragedy of their deaths. I bit down on my knuckles to stifle my sobs as my mind was in Lara's complete control, flooding my mind with snapshots of how that day had started; so full of promise for the future.

A gentle sea breeze wafted through the open window, causing the curtain to dance toward the bed, letting the warm amber light of the morning sun spill into the room. Her soft moans broke the morning stillness as she moved with a tenderness and affection that took my breath away. The warm glow on her flushed cheeks and the way her pink lips parted as she whispered her gratitude and declared her everlasting love for me was simply enchanting.

Her golden curls flowed gracefully over her soft, creamy skin, reminiscent of gentle waves lapping at the shore just a few kilometers away. As her pleasure grew, her eyes sparkled, and my name escaped her lips like a sweet melody while she collapsed onto me. The touch of her silky skin was a perfect contrast to my firm abs, creating an electric connection between us.

Her gaze lifted to meet mine, those striking blue eyes completely entrancing me. I gently tucked a stray lock of hair behind her ear to take in their beauty more fully, my heart racing in the wake of my own release. She appeared ethereal, with a porcelain-like complexion that was both fragile and exquisite.

As my hands cradled her curves, her soft, inviting lips brushed against mine in a playful manner. "Nico," she murmured, her lashes fluttering softly like the delicate wings of a butterfly. "There's something I need to share with you."

I felt a mix of confusion and intrigue as I noticed the fullness of her form. She let out a light laugh, using her hands to balance herself above me. "Nico, I'm pregnant."

My heart raced, feeling as if it might leap from my chest, overwhelmed by a surge of emotions. I wrapped my arms around her, driven by an instinct to shield her from harm. Our lips met in a passionate kiss, a testament to my unwavering love and commitment. A grin stretched across my face, reflecting the sheer joy bubbling within me.

"Lara," I whispered, gently shifting her off me to take in the subtle curve of her belly that I had just noticed. I placed soft kisses around the area that cradled our second child, my fingertips quivering as they glided over her skin. After years of longing for another little one, a sibling for Eve, it felt as if the goddess Aphrodite had finally smiled upon us.

Just then, the bedroom door swung open, and the gentle sound of my daughter's tiny feet on the cool tiles filled the air. She stood at the foot of the bed, a perfect miniature of her mother, with bouncy blonde curls and eyes sparkling like topaz.

With her head tilted curiously, she couldn't quite see our bare forms hidden beneath the blankets, her wide eyes sparkling with curiosity. "Mama? Papa?" she inquired, a big yawn escaping her lips. "Hug..." she whimpered, reaching her arms up toward us.

I couldn't help but laugh with joy at her presence, lifting her gently and placing her on the bed next to us. In that moment, my heart felt whole. Our little family of three was on the brink of becoming four. Lara's smile reflected my own as we took our time getting dressed, gazing out at the stunning scenery outside our bedroom window.

"Mama, us...boat?" I glanced at Lara, unsure, as she was far better at interpreting our four-year-old's chatter than I was.

Her eyes sparkled with mischief, "Yes sweetheart, all going on a boat today. Isn't that right, Eve?" She grinned widely, pulling out some ferry tickets from a drawer. "It was supposed to be a surprise. For your birthday."

Eve bounced on the bed, her face lighting up with pure joy. "Boat, boat, boat!" she exclaimed, her excitement spilling over. Her laughter echoed around us, filling my heart with warmth. It was her first time on a boat, her first adventure beyond the shores of the Greek island on which we lived.

Lara embraced me tightly, drawing my face closer to hers. The delightful scent of her floral perfume danced in the air, "I want your birthday to be nothing short of amazing."

A sharp, stabbing pain shot through my chest, forcing me to bend over. I struggled to breathe as it felt like my lungs were caught in a relentless grip. Aphrodite's neon sign flickered to life as I aimlessly strolled the coast towards it. Stopping to splash my face with the saltwater from the waves that crashed into my feet to wash away the tears that had started to roll down my cheeks.

We were enjoying delicious fresh omelets when the home phone suddenly rang. Since it was my birthday, I had the largest serving, piled high with grilled vegetables and sprinkled with grated cheese. Just as I was savoring a forkful, the piercing ring startled us all. "I'll get it," she said, already springing up from her seat.

Her eyes widened in shock as she looked at me from across the room, her complexion turning pale and drawn. "Nico..." she murmured, covering the mouthpiece with her hand. "It's about your father," she breathed, her lower lip quivering. "I'm so sorry, Nico."

A surge of anger coursed through me, marking the moment when the day began to sour. Everything that followed that phone call blurred into a painful memory, too raw and dreadful to dissect in detail. Just fragments were enough to send chills racing beneath my skin.

"Nico, I'm sorry, your father..."

"He was a heartless jerk." I retorted, immediately regretting my harshness. I reached for her hands, "Lara, darling, I apologize. He's just—"

"He's still your father, Nico. He loved you."

"He had a funny way of showing it."

She nodded, silently acknowledging my inner conflict. When she continued speaking, I found I was no longer listening, her words faded into the background. My father was gone. A heart attack had taken him. Andreas, his closest friend, had delivered the devastating news. "Nico, I need your help with the arrangements..." There was a long, uncomfortable silence before his voice trembled again. "Nico, you need to decide what to do with Aphrodite's."

Lara's gaze conveyed everything as she stood beside me, her arm gently resting on my shoulder. I let out a heavy sigh, saying, "Andreas, you know I could never part with it. His spirit would haunt me relentlessly, and I'd never find peace if I even considered it."

On the other end of the line, I caught a faint, almost instinctive chuckle. "Nico, you're a devoted son. But you know your mother... she's not in a condition to take over." I sighed again, pinching the bridge of my nose in frustration. The thought of my mother weighed heavily on my heart. She was deteriorating, her mind slowly succumbing to the shadows. First, it was her forgetfulness with daily tasks, and now her memories were slipping away, her words trapped in silence before they could escape. These days, she was hauntingly quiet, confined to a care home, barely clinging to life. I often wondered how long it would be before Death would finally grant her peace.

"And there's one more thing," he continued. "Today... I hate to ask, especially under the circumstances but I really need your assistance... we are down three servers and without your father-"

I swallowed hard, my gaze drifting to my pregnant wife and daughter. I could see her pacing, biting her nails. I felt torn between my responsibilities as a son and my role as a father and husband. She looked at me, her head was nodding yes, but I could see her trying to disguise the disappointment in her eyes. "It's fine. You should go," she whispered, not needing to hear the conversation to know what was being asked of me. That was what I loved about Lara; she was capable of reading people from their tone of their voice down to their body language. At times she seemed to know me better than I knew myself.

"Andreas, I'll be there." I said finally.

The consequences of those four words weighed heavily on my chest, causing my vision to blur and a wave of nausea to crash through me. When I finally composed myself, I was standing at the base of Aphrodite's. My feet had guided me here, where I stood alone once more. The decision I had made that day had forged this future; I had been the maker of my own misery.

I had held onto Lara's ghost tighter as the years went by. I could not accept the harsh reality that she was gone, that this lonely existence was my punishment for choosing the business over my family. The constant reminders that my whole world lay at the bottom of the ocean, taking with it any hope of happiness for my future.

I felt the grip of arms tightening around me like a serpent as I struggled against them. From my spot on Aphrodite's beach, I had seen the boat burst into flames on the water, my eyes locked on the distant horizon. A scream erupted from my throat, and my legs propelled me toward the ferry port. "LARA! EVE!" I yelled, forcing my way through the crowd that had gathered along the shore, morbidly fascinated by the unfolding disaster.

Their voices faded into a haunting silence, disbelief and terror painted across their faces. My heart pounded in my chest, my muscles protesting with every step, yet I pressed on until I reached them. Breathless and drenched in sweat, I fought through the throng at the marina, desperate to get as close as I could.

That was when the guards stopped me. "You can't go any further," one of them said. "There's nothing you can do to help; let the emergency services do their job," he insisted, as my frantic explanations spilled out.

I whimpered their names, but the guard remained unmoved. He was a short, balding man in his late fifties, a stark contrast to the towering, intimidating figure of my father.

A wave of crimson surged through my vision, fueled by the fury I felt towards the guard standing in my way. I had managed to slip free from the other guard's grip, my fist smashing into his face with a satisfying impact. He stumbled back, creating a brief opening as another guard rushed to assist him. I charged through that gap like a force of nature, pushing forward until I reached the dock's edge.

Suddenly, the ground seemed to vanish beneath me, and I plummeted, the encroaching darkness threatening to engulf me as I landed in a crumpled position on my knees. I fought to maintain my focus, watching as small lifeboats darted towards the raging inferno, shrinking into mere black dots against the horizon in their desperate attempt to reach the flames.

The sky darkened with thick, black smoke, heavy and sticky as the wind carried it across the landscape, smothering the Grecian sun and chilling the air. Ashes drifted down like bitter snowflakes.

I stood there for what felt like an eternity, anxiously awaiting any news, my eyes fixed on the boat. I watched in grotesque horror as it sank into the ocean, torn apart into two halves by the flames that had consumed its center. In mere minutes, the twisted wreckage vanished beneath the waves. As I watched the sea engulf both halves of the vessel, time seemed to slow to a crawl. The knot in my stomach tightened, I could feel the ache in my bones and their absence in my inanimate heart - Lara and Eve were dead. They had been taken from me by Hephaetus' wrath, though I did not know what anyone on board that ship could have done to have deserved the Greek god of Fire's punishment.

Along the dock, relatives of other passengers gathered, their faces etched with disbelief. A chorus of muffled sobs filled the air as a guard approached us. His grave expression spoke volumes, confirming the fears that had taken root in our hearts. I barely caught his words: "No survivors. The storm... the waves were too fierce... we couldn't risk more lives... it's impossible to recover any bodies."

A raw, animalistic wail erupted from deep within me, echoing across the still deserted beach. My body shook uncontrollably. I recalled my father's insensitive and heartless words once more. *"Remember Nico, boys don't cry."*

It had been his mantra in keeping people out and shielding his emotions from the world, it seemed to have worked for him. I eagerly adopted it, or tried to, since that tragic day in the hope that by shutting the world out I would save myself from enduring any more pain.

That was when I caught a glimpse of Andreas out of the corner of my eye, stood in the door of the restaurant, beside him was Cali. Even though I could not see her fully from here, the memories from last night flooded through my mind. *How had she managed to get here before me?* I glanced at my watch, almost an hour had passed without noticing.

Lara's icy grip relinquished, disappearing quickly as Cali made her way over to me. The last chink of my armor fell. I yearned to embrace her, but I drew in a deep breath and pushed it down. *No strings attached.* I told myself.

"Nico... are you okay?" She asked, her hand touching the same spot Lara's ghost had clung to. I nodded, swallowing the lump in the back of my throat. "Is it about... we can, um, forget anything ever happened, if that's what you want?" she said quietly, her eyes cast down to her feet as she dropped her arm to her side.

I nodded, "I think that would be for the best."

The possessive beast within me stirred as I watched Cali walk away from me, her head bowed as she pushed forward and away from the restaurant. My hands balled into fists as I shoved them into my pockets. *She is mine,* it snarled. *I refuse to lose her because I cannot let go of the past.*

"Cali... wait." I called, but she continued to walk away, refusing to give me another backwards glance.

Fourteen

Cali

I knew this had all been a bad idea; *Nico, the villa, coming back to Rhodes*. I should be with the one person who needed me, the one person I could truly rely on: my mom. I should not be pining after a man I barely knew. I had known sleeping with him was going to be a mistake; I was not the type of person to have sex with no feelings. Yet I did it anyway. So, it was my own fault that my emotions were all over the place. Now there was no turning back; he wanted to forget it happened and I had to live with his rejection. *Perhaps it is for the best; rebound flings never end well.*

I slammed the villa door shut behind me, curling into a ball on the couch, draping the thin cotton blanket around me, feeling white hot tears sting my eyes. *I would not be feeling this way if Adam had been loyal. We would be sipping chilled champagne and enjoying this beautiful villa together, happily married and in love.*

Laying there in the silence with only the faint thrum of the swimming pool filter buzzing through the open window, Adam and Steph were the star performers in the adult show that played in my head. *How long had they been fucking behind my back?* A bitter taste lingered in my mouth as I wondered what the two of them were doing now. *Are they happy that I am no longer in their way?*

The thought of the two of them together churned my stomach, their symphony of moans and grunts echoed in my mind, provoking my tears until they cascaded down my face. *Why am I not enough? Why Stephanie?* Without my best friend as well as my fiancé, I had no one. Nor did I have a cell phone to call the hospital to talk to my mom. Not that I would tell her what happened of course, but just hearing her voice would have soothed me.

Two days had passed since Nico's rejection. I had used those days to discover other areas of Rhodes as I tried to keep myself busy and my mind distracted. Trying to do all I could to avoid Aphrodite's, to avoid *Nico*. Slowly trying to whittle down my time here before my return flight back to the United States; back to watching my mother suffer - wishing that everything was different.

I had thought perhaps a quick meaningless fuck with the handsome hunk would take my mind off Adam, at least momentarily. Allowing my lust to devour him and to consume me fully was the distraction I so desperately needed. Instead, it had ignited a fire that sizzled and scorched my veins. Now every fiber in my body longed for his touch. I knew my feelings ran deep, deeper than his ever would for me but his rejection had stung. It had broken me to hear that once again I was not good enough.

The morning sunlight filtered in through the blinds, falling onto the note Nico had left. His number written in his slanted scrawl taunted me as I sat on the edge of the bed staring at it. *Why had he left me his number?*

I crumpled up the note angrily, launching it across the room. *I should have listened to Andreas.* I had played with fire and gotten burned. *And I have no one but myself to blame.*

I got to my feet, annoyed with myself for entertaining even the slightest idea that sleeping with Nico would have made me feel better. Clearly, I was a master of my own destruction; willingly entering the lion's den as a vulnerable lamb. Even as I showered, trying to push all thoughts of Nico out of my mind, I could not help but recall the way he made me feel. I wanted him to punish my body with his brutish ways, to feel his hands wrap around my throat and fuck me until I could no longer think straight.

Jealousy flooded me at the thought of him being with another woman these past few days; an emotion I had never entertained in the past. I had been safe and confident in the knowledge that Adam was mine, that nothing or no one could have ever come between us, could ever sway his affections. *How naïve I had been.* I wanted Nico all to myself to love and fuck to my heart's content. I did not want any other woman enjoying his touch.

I looked at the clock, the hour hand resting on three. At this early time Nico would be getting ready to start his day. I imagined his muscular torso still adorned with my deep scratches pulling on a cotton shirt, his lips pulled into a lazy smile as he embraced another new day - hiding the pain he felt behind it.

Butterflies fluttered in my stomach at the thought of him, but he had made it crystal clear. I meant nothing. Upon re-entering the bedroom my eyes caught the scrunched-up piece of paper with Nico's number on it; a moment of weakness overcame me as I scooped it off the floor. It trembled in my hand as I placed it back on the bedside table before getting dressed.

A fierce determination spread through my body as I stared at my reflection. *I will not let Nico ruin the last few days here in Rhodes,* I thought. *I came to see Andreas, to persuade him to visit my mom while he still could.*

"I always loved your long hair" I heard Adam's voice echo in my mind as I brushed through the damp strands of my hair. *"It makes you look so innocent and pure."* A smirk crept on my face as I took hold of the scissors. *Not anymore, sunshine.*

Adam's imaginary voice begged me to stop, but only once the floor surrounding my feet was littered with long lengths of my dark, glossy hair did I stop to admire my handiwork. I shook my head from side to side, reveling in the feel of the short tendrils as they grazed my jawline. *No man will ever make me feel like shit again.*

An unexpected knock on the villa door startled me. I rushed to the door, my short hair feeling light and featherlike as it whipped at my face. I swung open the door expecting to see the holiday rep - she had told me to expect her visit a day or so before I was checking out. Instead, a bunch of flowers and a card was left on the doorstep. Snatching up the card, my eyes scanned it recognizing the slanted scrawl instantly.

Thea, I miss you.
Please join me for breakfast.

Flecks of crimson and gold danced in the sky. The scene was breathtaking as I walked beneath it, my body abuzz with excitement. It was silly how a small note and some flowers could change my mood; but each step I took I felt my smile widen across my face at the thought of seeing Nico once more.

My stomach growled hungrily as I thought of my favorite breakfast dish; Greek bougatsa, wondering how Andreas' compared to my mother's delicious homemade version. It had been some time since I had tasted it, but the mere idea of the delicate, golden-brown puff pastry drenched in sweet honey made my mouth water.

The neon sign of Aphrodite's was not yet switched on and the sunbeds lay untouched, waiting to be arranged neatly under the straw umbrellas. *I am too early*, I thought, as I wandered towards the beach, noticing a small yellow bucket that caught my attention.

It took me back to my childhood, reminiscent of a castle-shaped bucket with four charming turrets at each corner, remembering the many summer holidays I had spent on this beach with my father building sandcastles.

I sank to my knees beside the bucket, momentarily transported back to those carefree days of my youth; reliving those happy memories as I scooped the sand inside the bucket. Forgetting for those few moments that I was now a grown woman. A woman filled with desire for a man whose heart was as unyielding as his physique.

Fifteen

Nico

Sandcastles, three of them, dotted beside her, each one deformed and crumbling. I observed her for a while, sensing her frustration as her fourth creation collapsed almost instantly. For a brief moment, I had not recognized her with her cropped hair and the dim glow of the early hour. She was sitting cross-legged on the pale sand, her khaki dress fanned out behind her. She exuded a captivating allure that gripped my insides like a vice. *I was so sure that she would not come.*

I paused, holding my breath as I moved cautiously, unable to believe she was truly there. For so long I have lived among ghosts and false visions of hope that it took several moments to fully accept that Cali was there waiting for me.

I had taken a longer route back from her villa, trying to shake off Lara's ghost that followed me like an ominous black cloud. For the first time in over seven years, I resented my own inability to move on, to let her ghost rest. I had clung to her, wanting to keep her alive in any way possible, manifesting her ethereal form. Now though, I was unable to get her to leave.

As I had walked through the streets, I had wondered whether Cali would have been awake; the villa had been dark and the curtains were drawn. I cursed myself for not waiting for her to answer, but I was a coward. *What if she did not feel the same way?*

As I approached Aphrodite's there was a shadow hunched over on the sand - a woman. I had not recognized her at first because of the dramatic haircut; but I knew that figure well. Every curve etched into my skin from my hours of exploration. *Cali is waiting for me.*

Yet, seeing her waiting for me, her prompt response from receiving my flowers, I knew there had to be something more, something deeper, than just the physical connection between us. I shuffled closer, the fabric of my shorts tightening around the crotch as my eyes cast over her, catching the delectable floral scent from her skin. I found myself staring at her shorter hair, initially unsure if I liked it; but with it she emanated a confidence she never had before. Cali was beautiful, she could be bald and I still would be attracted to her.

Her white cotton dress fanned out behind her, and I could tell from her profile that she was not wearing a bra, her perky nipples standing hard beneath the fabric. I wanted to run my thumb over them, to encompass them with my mouth.

"Nico?" she asked, scrambling to her feet, brushing the sand off of her bare legs. I watched as the dress tumbled past her knees, swaying delicately in the gentle breeze brought inland by the tide. She looked unsure as she tentatively stepped towards me, wringing her fingers and biting her lip.

"Cali" I smiled as I began to walk in her direction. "I wasn't sure if you would come." She stopped a few feet from me, her dark brown eyes sparkling in the dim glow of the streetlight behind me. "Cali... I was a jerk-"

Suddenly, Cali launched herself toward me, her arms wrapping around my neck and her lips locking onto mine. She took me by surprise and I found my thoughts slipping out of my mouth faster than I could regret hearing them echo in the silence that enveloped us. "Cali, I have missed you. I haven't been able to stop thinking about you... I was a prick-"

Her warm, minty breath flitted across my face as she let out a small chuckle flitted across my face. "You said it was for the best-" She gasped breathlessly before I silenced her with another kiss, my hand roaming in the soft tendrils of her hair, allowing the silkiness to slip through my fingers before clasping it tightly in a fist and pulling her body closer to mine.

"I was wrong." My voice sounded more serious, more intense than I had intended. My eyes scanned the beach, it was still too early for anyone else to arrive. I smirked, as I pulled her dress over her head in one swift movement; enjoying the way her breasts bounced deliciously with her hard peaks for nipples exposed. I eyed the rest of her body wearing nothing but a pair of white lacy thongs. *I want her now,* I thought as my free hand slid down the small of her back, pressing her hips into the bulge that was raging a war in my shorts.

"I have missed you too." Cali purred, grinding her hips against me, her white lace underwear driving me wild. As my fingertips brushed the waistline. I tugged at them wanting to rip them away from her body and bury myself deep inside her. Her lips parted as she moaned, grinding herself against my engorged shaft.

"I need you." I told her, suddenly breaking apart and clutching her wrist, dragging her to the coastline.

I felt Cali tense as the icy cold water nipped at her toes, "I will keep you warm." I promised, my eyes following her every move as she stepped out of her lace thong and followed me deeper into the ocean until her delicious body was swallowed by the waves. "Thea" I purred as I drew her near me, encouraging her legs to wrap around my waist.

The possessive beast within me stirred as my hands roamed her body, feeling goosebumps prickle our skin like thousands of small needles as the cold bit deep into our bones. The only thing that was warm was her heat as she slid down my length, as her kisses as our mouths locked together once more. "Thea" I repeated over and over, digging my fingers deeper into her fleshy thighs.

I felt her muscles tense, heard her moans whimper in my ear and was almost strangled by her arms as they tightened around my neck. "Nico... I'm so close." She whimpered, her words dancing across my lips. I thrust with all the energy I had, demonstrating just how much I have missed this, missed *her*, these past couple of days.

I could feel my load swell in my balls as she teetered on the brink of her climax. "Thea, I have to tell you something." I whispered in her ear. "You are not like the other women. You are something else..." My kisses grew more frantic as I felt her inner walls close in around my shaft, "I want you to know... I haven't been with anyone since..." I growled, sinking my lips into the nape of her neck as my own impending release drew closer. "Cali... I only want you... *I want to make you mine.*" The last few words came out in a snarl, unable to shield the possessiveness that seeped into my voice.

Calli remained silent, biting on her bottom lip, stifling her cries as she climaxed. Her whole body shook matching the rhythmic pulsations on her core. Three twitches was all it took to take me with her as my load erupted, pushing even deeper with each forceful jet that filled her with my seed.

Breathless and gasping she looked at me, her pupils widened in the hazy light. "Nico, I..." she paused, slowly unwinding her legs from my waist, but keeping her body close to me. I could feel her heart beating rapidly in her chest. Her eyes flitted across my face as her satisfied smile curled at her lips and her arms tightened around my torso.

A lump formed in the back of my throat and a pit opened up inside my stomach. I knew it was impulsive, possessive, selfish but I *needed* her. "*Thea*," I murmured nuzzling her neck until I heard her soft shallow breaths once more, hearing the words I have been desperate to hear.

"I am yours... if you want me."

Sixteen

Cali

My chest tightened and my stomach lurched as I spent the day loitering around Aphrodite's. Guilt flooded me every time I caught Nico's eye, catching the glimmer of happiness that lurked in them. I forced a small smile on my face, I was set to return to the US in two days and neither Andreas or Nico knew. I had been so desperate in my desire to return, yet now I wished I had not changed my flights. I had felt like a failure and a fraud as I had walked through the busy city, stopping in a local coffeehouse and using their old PC to sign into the travel agents website.

I convinced myself that it was the right thing to do - I had failed in my mission to convince Andreas to visit my mom, unable to break through his stubborn dislike of Americans to make my dying mother's wish a reality. I had also told myself that leaving here, leaving Nico, would be easier sooner rather than later. That was until this morning. My bottom lip quivered; *how can I leave now?*

"Cali, is everything alright?" Andreas asked, sitting beside me on the sunbed. I shook my head, averting my gaze to the floor. My head was a tangled web of thoughts that I could not make sense of.

"I need my mom." I muttered, the truth of it hit me in the chest. *She is the only person who would understand.* My hands clenched into balls as I tried to fight back the tears. "I don't know what I will do when she..." my voice broke as the sobs I had been holding back all day shook my body. "I shouldn't have come here... It's clear I have failed her uncle..."

Andreas' arms embraced me, holding me and allowing my tears to soak the shoulder of his shirt. "I have spoken to your mother every day Cali, since you have been here," he said softly, "She made me promise not to say anything to you... she wanted you to relax and enjoy yourself." His smile crept across his face, deep lines creased at the corners of his eyes. "I have to apologize to you Cali... what I said, it was out of line. But I also must thank you... if you never came here, I never would have spoken to Loretta again" He sighed, "I am *truly* sorry that I cannot see her once more." His voice cracked.

We sat in silence for a few moments before Andreas finally broke the silence. "I think this has more to do with a certain bar owner." He smirked. "That perhaps you have developed feelings for him you were not prepared for, especially given the situation with your ex-fiancé."

I sniffed, burying my head deeper into his shoulder. "Cali, I have never seen Nico as happy in these past few years as I have since you have been here, especially this morning..."

I stared at him. "But uncle... I have to go home..." He nodded, slowly pulling me away from him, holding my shoulders as he stared into my eyes.

"You both have to be honest... what do both of you truly want?"

"Thea? What's wrong?" Nico's voice suddenly sounded, startling me. I swiped at my tears, shaking my head.

"Nothing, it's nothing." I whimpered, turning away from them both. I concentrated on putting one foot in front of the other, keeping my head forward. Emotions fizzling inside wanting to erupt at any moment.

Nico's firm hand caught hold of my wrist, spinning me around to face him. "Thea, talk to me." His voice was firm but his fingertips traced the side of my face gently. His thumb brushed at a tear that silently rolled down my cheek.

"What do you want from me Nico - from *us*?"

Seventeen

Nico

There was not a moment to spare, our kisses were intense and passionate as we fumbled through the villa ripping items of clothing off until we were in the kitchen naked and panting with delirious lust. "Nico" she murmured as her soft breasts crushed against my chest.

With ease, I lifted her up onto the cool marble worktop. I kissed her neck, feeling the raised bumps against my tongue, tasting the salt on her skin and smelling her enchanting perfume. I needed her, wanted her, in every way she would give herself to me.

I spread her legs wide, her smooth pussy glistened, inviting me to taste it. Without a moment's hesitation, my mouth was there between her silky thighs, her hands tangled in my hair, holding my head in place. With eager, passionate flicks, my tongue danced against her, knowing exactly what sent her over the edge. I curled my tongue against her inner folds in rapid strokes, I savored every drop, intent on coaxing out more of her sweet nectar.

"Come for me," the demanding beast within me purred, "Your orgasms are mine... *You* are mine."

As her moans grew louder, the knuckles of her hand gripping the counter turned white. "Nico," she gasped, beads of sweat glistened like delicate pearls between her breasts. "I'm going to—"

Warm, sticky bursts of her sweetness filled my mouth as I hungrily devoured her, the taste of her spread across my tongue, filling my mouth with a perfect blend of sweet and salty flavors almost reminiscent of a rich salted caramel.

"How... did you do... *that?*" she panted, her face flushed, a flicker of embarrassment etched on her face as she tried to clamp her thighs shut. I held her legs open, my tongue darting in and out of her entrance, teasing out another wave of pleasure. I looked up at her with a smirk, her juices coating my chin. Her eyes darkened, and an animalistic growl escaped her as she thrust my head back to the treasure that lay awaiting for me. With each flick of my tongue against her engorged clit and coaxing my fingers deep inside her I felt her body relax, deep thrusts inside her tight entrance, her head lolled backwards as she surrendered herself fully to me.

Over and over, I took her beyond any pleasure she had felt before. I was driven to please her; all I wanted was for her to know how special she was - to make her as happy as she made me.

The sounds of leaves rustling outside caught my attention, but she yanked on my hair, shoving my face back to her pussy. I thought I heard footsteps but they were soon drowned out by her loud squeal as every muscle in her body tensed as another orgasm crashed through her, flooding the counter with her delicious nectar.

Cali pulled me up to her height, her tongue lapping up her own cum, tasting herself on my lips. Our kisses became fierce, powerful, *unstoppable* as she savored the flavor of her cream. "Nico," she whispered softly, her breath smelled of her sweetness. "I want to repay the favor."

My arousal surged to a deeper, unknown level, as I observed her graceful, fluid-like movements as she descended from the counter to kneel at my feet. Her captivating gaze held mine, filled with allure and vigor as her lips enveloped me instantly.

Leaning back against the sink, a low groan escaped me and my pulse quickened as her hands wrapped around my member.

The worktop pressed uncomfortably into my back, but I was no longer able to comprehend pain, only pleasure. I was completely overwhelmed by her remarkable technique as her hands pumped along my shaft, cupping my balls before her tongue skillfully navigated the sensitive purple engorged tip. She greedily lapped up the precum that oozed from it as if it was her favorite flavor of ice-cream.

A shadow crossed the room, but my mind could not concentrate on what had caused it, as my cock jerked in delight. I felt her mouth create a perfect seal around me. Cali thrust her face towards the base of my shaft, moving up and down my length with a zealous passion. The intensity continued to build within me, my skin sizzled with excitement as she took me to the apex of my release. The anticipation to spend my load in that pretty mouth of hers riled me up until my thrusts grew harder and more intense. Sinking it deeper until it hit the back of her throat.

The villa was silent apart from the soft, glorious sounds of her gagging and the sound of my balls slapping her chin as I fucked those plump lips. I noticed another shadow out the corner of my eye and I attempted to turn to see what had caused it but Cali's grip tightened on my thighs, holding me in place.

Cali's wide, innocent eyes were fixed on me, but I was not deceived by her coy facade. I knew there was a dark side of her, seeing her for the beautiful seductress that she truly was.

I drove my shaft as deep as I could before my load exploded like a thousand fireworks. She gulped as much of my load as she could, before I pulled out and covered her gorgeous face with the sticky streams.

My breathing ragged, I pulled her up to her feet, my fingers brushed the side of her face, watching as my seed trickled down her cheeks, dribbling onto her perky breasts. "Beautiful," I whimpered, feeling my vulnerability break through to the surface. I had never called anyone other than Lara beautiful. But seeing this woman in my arms, her face and body marked by my seed - it was a sight that I never wanted to forget.

It satisfied my possessive beast seeing her covered in my essence, tasting it and *enjoying* it. I scooped a blob of it onto my fingertip, purring as she sucked it clean. Unable to control myself I spun her around and bent her over the kitchen island, forcing everything on top of it out of the way in my haste. The glass fruit bowl shattered on the floor, as apples and oranges tumbled and rolled across the tiled floor.

Cali presented her round ass to me, the only place I was yet to fully explore. Wiggling it before me as a seductive invitation. I grabbed each cheek in my hands, spreading them wide, revealing her tight rosebud entrance, begging to be filled. Without hesitation my mouth descended upon it, teasing her tight entrance with my tongue, evoking animalistic sounds from Cali as I slowly entered a finger as my others drove deep into her soaking wet slit. She bucked against them, matching my pace, urging me to insert another, to stretch her holes as much as she could handle.

My cock rose to the challenge, as I pressed the tip against her slit, two fingers still lodged in her ass, She squealed loudly and her fingers clawed at the edges of the counter, bracing herself for the rest of my shaft. "That's a good girl." I murmured the moment her ass cheeks smacking against my thighs as I drove into her, knowing my cum still streaked her face. Watching her side profile as her tongue darted to the corner of her mouth collecting a globule of cum that collected there. Her body convulsed, caught amid her throes of pleasure, her voice quivering as she called out my name as I continued to fuck her through another orgasm.

Her slender fingers loosened momentarily on around the edge of the counter, almost docile as she rode the wave of her pleasure, but not yet completely satisfied as she pressed herself back into my cock deep inside her slit, forcing my fingers to penetrate her ass even deeper.

Our bodies collided with the rhythmic clapping sound, followed by our crescendo of our harmonious groans and whispers. I felt her muscles tense, her legs trembling like jelly as I wrapped one hand around her throat, squeezing just enough for her to know she was mine. Only mine.

Her bottom lip trembled, her voice a warbled sigh as she climaxed, her nectar gushed from her entrance soaking me and pooling on the tiles at my feet. Her body collapsed fully on the counter; her breasts crushed beneath her because her arms were too weak to hold her quaking body as the orgasm ripped through her.

My free hand ran up her spine, before grabbing hold of a fistful of her hair and yanking her back upright. "I am not finished with you yet." I told her, hearing her whimper slightly as she summoned the strength to resume her position. I slowly removed my fingers, watching her tight asshole gape ever so slightly. Cali shuddered, as I replaced them with the tip of my shaft; drenched in her cum, using it like a lubricant to ease my length inside. Her knuckles turned white as she moaned through her obvious pain.

"Cali," I groaned, unable to hold back any longer, the tightness of its embrace around my cock had me closer to the edge than anticipated. "Have you ever been fucked like this?" A jealousy washed over me, not wanting to hear anything other than 'no' come from her lips. *This was mine, no one is allowed to touch it, or her, for that matter.*

She shook her head, taking deep breaths as I worked her hole with the entire length of my shaft.

"Nico... I've never-" She took a sharp intake of breath. I watched her body crumple forward onto the counter, crushing her bare breasts once more, my cock slid as deep as it could go. "Does it still hurt?" I asked her, my fingers reaching around to her slit, driving three fingers inside her without warning. She thrust her fist to her mouth stifling her screams.

"I want you to enjoy this *Thea*" I purred, my thumb stroking her clit in slow, tantalizing circles. "I want to fill your ass with the last of my cum." Another whimper, this one of pleasure, as her resistance eased, my own moan of pleasure resonated from my chest as her tight, unexplored entrance yielded to me fully, allowing me to fuck her harder and faster than before.

She removed the fist from her mouth, revealing the crimson bite marks etched on her knuckles. Pushing her ass back against me, giving my other hand more room to spread her slit wider, my knuckles smashing into her with a vigor.

"Harder Nico," she whispered, trying to turn her head to face me, fire burning in her eyes. "I can take it."

I growled, digging my fingers into her hips, rocking her hips harder against mine, slamming her ass cheeks against my thighs with such force my hands left imprints and her ass cheeks were red. Pressure was building inside of her like a shaken soda bottle, I could feel it thrum beneath her skin and I heard the quiver in her throaty growl. Caving into her carnal desires as the intensity of her climax overwhelmed her. Her body writhed and bucked in response forcing the counter to cut into her stomach.

"Fuck" I murmured as both her tight holes pulsated, gripping my cock and my fingers in their vice-like grip. Her cum made a sopping wet mess of everything; coating my fingers and flowing down her creamy thighs. The sound of it splattering against the terracotta tiles, combined with her ecstatic scream, pushed me to the brink of ecstasy.

It left me breathless, as I clung to her, shooting my load deep into her ass. My thick, sticky ropes clung to her skin and trickled out of her holes as I gradually withdrew. I stared at it for a moment, fascinated by the sight of my final claim on her body.

"Nico," she gasped, "that was—" But before she could finish, she froze in shock, her expression instantly shifted to horror. I followed her line of vision seeing a silhouette of a man in the window watching us.

The door burst open, slamming into the wall, the squeals of protest from its hinges pierced the silence. Revealing an ominous shadow standing before us. A pair of deep blue eyes pierced mine from beneath a fringe of blond floppy hair that clung to his unshaven face with sweat.

I felt her body move faster than lightning, her hands quick to retrieve the fluffy white towel that had slid off of her curvaceous body during our encounter. Her whole body shook, but out of fear not pleasure. The fire that had once danced in her eyes snuffed out in an instant.

She choked on his name as it clogged the back of her throat, "Adam?"

Eighteen

Cali

I felt the fire in my cheeks ignite as I lunged for the towel that had fallen to the floor, I wiped my face before wrapping it tightly around my body. I was beyond mortified but my actions were lazy in my docile state. My thoughts were all over the place, still experiencing the high from my intense climax.

Beads of sweat clung to my skin, and my eyes were wide with panic, the sudden jolt from my ecstasy had me feeling like a deer caught in the glare of oncoming headlights. I could feel my fight or flight instinct kicking in, but there was nowhere to run and I definitely could not hide.

The shadow cleared its throat, pointing to my face. "I think you missed some." The words were as cold as steel, when he spoke. His voice was instantly recognizable; a voice I had listened to for eight years tell me he loves me. *Now he is telling me to wipe another man's cum off of my face.*

"Adam?" His name was sharp and scratchy as it left my mouth, leaving a bitter aftertaste as I scrubbed at my face in the corner of the towel.

My gaze flicked toward the door, but his imposing and unyielding presence stood in the way of my escape. My heart pounded wildly in my chest, and my hands struggled to maintain a steady hold on the towel. Anger simmered just beneath the surface, ready to explode from the wound Adam had etched into my heart.

"Adam? What the *fuck* are you doing here?" My words filled with hate, angry at his intrusion. I was not going to allow him to make me feel embarrassed or ashamed. *I am not the one in the wrong here.*

Everything I had once loved about him I now despised. His blond floppy hair made him look like a child, his azure blue eyes now reminded me of his ice-cold heart.

On the outside he looked calm and composed, and showed no flicker of emotion, yet the air around him pulsed with intense fury. There was a moment in my life when I found his unyielding poker face captivating and enigmatic. My relentless curiosity and probing nature wrestled with the challenge of uncovering his genuine emotions, but I failed every time.

As he faced me, a powerful instinct surged within me to aim for his weak spot, the very source of the irreparable wounds he had inflicted on my heart.

I craved to see a spark of emotion, any sign of feeling flicker across his face. So, when his jaw tensed and his fists balled at his sides as he caught sight of Nico's still erect cock, glistening with our combined cum, my mouth curled into a smirk.

I held no guilt or regret for the chaos he had stumbled into; I wanted him to experience pain, to feel rage. Nothing he could endure now would ever match the torment he had caused me.

"Cali, we need to talk." His tone was harsh, sending a shiver along my spine. I could feel his gaze shift from my towel-clad body, which offered little coverage, to the white streak of Nico's release that trickled down my legs.

A jolt of electricity shot through my body as I stared at Adam; transporting me back in time. There I was, in the church, witnessing his affair unfold before my very eyes. He never even gave me a second thought, he never cared for me, never *loved* me. I was his safety net; the woman who had the role but never truly played the part.

As my *ex*-fiancé stood before me, the weight of his stare was oppressive and hateful. It was the first time in eight years I felt I had truly understood his emotions. *I hate him, so why does their betrayal still hurt so much?*

Adam stepped closer, revealing his slitted eyes and his vicious snarl. "Cali, *my love,* I had come here to talk about us." His gaze darted to Nico, rolling his eyes in annoyance as he observed him hurriedly pulling on his shorts. "You know she still loves me, don't you?" he asked Nico.

Do I still love him? Does my heart still ache for him even though he played me for a fool? I looked at Nico, feeling my body fill with warmth as his soft caramel eyes swept over my face. Kind and compassionate, a disbelieving look in his eyes as he ignored Adam and put his sole focus on me. *No. I don't love Adam, at least not any more.*

"I thought I would give you some space for a few days, you know...to calm down, so that we could discuss this like adults." His glare followed Nico, watching through slitted eyes as Nico draped his arm over my shoulder pulling me into him. Nico was giving Adam a warning - staking his claim on me.

Nico did not need to say a word, his actions had said it all; loud and clear for even someone like Adam to understand. *I am his.* It was clear in his body language; the way his face was nuzzled into my hair and the way he held himself so cool and confident showed that nothing Adam could say would make him relinquish his grasp on me.

Adam stroked his chin thoughtfully, his knuckles still pale from the tension of his clenched fists, while a prominent vein pulsed angrily at his temple. His composure was slipping. For once things were not going in his favor.

A sneer contorted his face, until I could no longer see what I had once found attractive about him. "I didn't have you down as a whore, fucking anything with a pulse," he hissed.

I felt Nico's mouth slip down to my ear, his words so quiet I barely heard them. "We had better not tell him about the *hairbrush*." He chuckled, his arm squeezing me tighter as my blush grew darker.

The sound of Adam's trainers squeaking against the terracotta tiles pierced the silence; each step extending the agonizing tension in the room. I wished he would just leave, to fuck off out of my life for good. Yet my words jammed in my throat, my bravado slowly ebbing away the longer Adam stood in front of us.

Suddenly, Adam stopped pacing, pivoting sharply to face me. His stare pierced through me like a thousand sharp blades. "I thought you of all people would have wanted to save our relationship... but I guess you haven't done much *thinking* since you have been here..."

His words stung. I recoiled as they hit me square in the chest, tearing at the wounds that had just started to heal. I could not let him wear me down, I would not cower to his masochistic arrogance and narcissistic manipulation. *Did he think I would wallow in self-pity and wait for him to return to me?*

"Fuck off Adam," I mumbled, my eyes fixed on the ground. My voice was strained but my tone was unmistakably sharp. "You don't even have the decency to apologize." I hissed, feeling my pulse throb and my anger seep through my pores. "So why did you really come here?"

Silence enveloped us all and, in that stillness, the unspoken words resonated more powerfully than any words in that instant, Nico's hand slipping into mine and interlocking his fingers showed our union. "I think you should leave." Nico said in his assertive and commanding voice, loosening his grip as he slowly stepped into the gap between Adam and I. His body shielding me from Adam's repugnant glare. "Before I *make you* leave."

My heart raced wildly as images of a confrontation flashed through my mind, yet Adam merely laughed. "I'll go when I am ready to leave, after all, I'm the one who paid for *all* of this...I have provided you with a place for you to fuck my fiancée."

"Ex-fiancée." I sneered as violent streaks of red tinged my vision and my fury consumed me. I side-stepped Nico and charged at Adam, my fists swinging wildly in the air. I clawed at every inch of his body that was within reach. For a few moments I had lost control. Enjoying the small thrill of satisfaction each time my fists landed a punch or my nails gouged at his flesh.

Nico's strong arms wrapped around me, holding me back from Adam, who remained frustratingly unfazed. I felt Nico whispering soothing words in my ear, though I paid little attention. *I wanted him to hurt, to feel a fraction of the pain I felt inside. Why could I never make him feel any sort of emotion?*

I was breathless, trembling as adrenaline pumped through my veins, I felt Adam's silent mocking eyes, as visions of Stephanie and him together haunted me, I had been completely oblivious to their twisted betrayal for so long.

Blood trickled from the gash on Adam's upper lip where my fist had first made contact, along with angry red scratches along his face. Nico's grip tightened on me, his lips brushed the top of my head, refusing to let go. "Cali, he's not worth it."

Adam's face twisted into a sinister grin as he wiped at the blood with the back of his hand. "Cali, I actually came here to tell you in person that a 'congratulations' is in order." He sneered, "I thought you would be happy that your best friend is pregnant." he said, his eyes lit up knowing he now had my full attention. "All those years thinking that *I* was never going to be a father... trying to console you and your *failures*."

Brushing nonexistent dust from his clothes, he continued to taunt me, reveling in the pain he was about to unleash. His sadistic smirk reminded me of a kid with a magnifying glass, burning poor defenseless ants on a hot summer's day. He was looking for my weaknesses, and he knew my infertility was my biggest one. I could see he was taking great pleasure in watching my face crumple, picking at the wound that refused to heal.

No longer able to look at him, my gaze dropped to the floor, as he said the words that shattered my soul. "Steph and I are starting *a family*, Cali... something *we* could never have. Something I have wanted my whole life. Of course there was no way *you* could never compare to *her*."

My eyes snapped up to him, my mind internally correcting him. *Our home*, I thought, *that bastard is going to move her into our home.* I pulled my mouth into a tight line, refusing to rise to his bait. Even though I could feel white-hot tears pricking my eyes and threatening to erupt at any given moment. I wiped them away. My mouth parched and raw, as if my own words were sharp blades tearing at my throat. "Go rot in Hell, Adam."

I had struggled to maintain a fierce gaze as the tears started to roll down my cheeks, watching as he slowly backed out of the door silently with a lingering smirk on his face. Nico tried to pull me into a hug, but as soon as the door slammed shut behind Adam, I fled to the bathroom.

My bare feet slapping against the cold, hard tiles, matching the furious beat that my heart had become and tasting bile in the back of my throat.

My shoulders slumped; my whole body curled in on itself as the tears poured down my face. I crumpled into a heap over the toilet bowl as the room around me spun.

"Cali," Nico's gentle voice called out, kneeling beside me, wrapping me in the warmth of his compassion like a cozy blanket. His hands tenderly held my hair back. "He's a real nasty piece of shit," he murmured, offering me a bottle of water he had brought in from the kitchen. He had opened it before handing it over to me. I sipped at it, but it felt like I was swallowing vinegar, scorching my insides as it mixed with the bile that was lodged in the back of my throat.

"He never deserved you," he declared with a passion that made my heart race. In that instant, I experienced a surreal moment, like a cartoon character caught mid-run, suspended in the air with no ground beneath them. We all know they will eventually fall, but not the cartoon. Not until it's too late.

My heart felt like it was hanging in the balance, teetering on the edge of a fall into the deep chasm of the unknown that I was not prepared to face. It clung to Nico, longing for him as fiercely as every other part of me did. Despite my uncle's caution, I found myself falling hopelessly in love with Nico Karamanlis.

Time seemed to freeze; the only sound was the gentle rush of blood in my ears, accompanied by the warmth of Nico's hand resting on the small of my back. The wave of nausea had faded, but I still felt an emptiness inside, my lower abdomen tightening, a reminder that this was the closest I would ever come to experiencing labor pains.

"Cali," he whispered into my shoulder, his teeth grazing my skin, igniting a spark that sent waves of pleasure through me. My body responded with an explosion of sensations, and I felt myself surrender completely as he filled me. Our breaths intertwined heavily, hearts racing in unison as we pressed against each other, lost in the moment. "All I want is *you.*"

Nineteen

Nico

The moment our bodies intertwined, I was caught off guard by the sudden rush of blood that filled my head and made my pulse throb in my temples. The need to make her feel wanted, special, *mine*. Her fingertips ran along my spine, my flesh tingled under her touch, leaving goosebumps in their wake. This was more than lust; it had been from the moment I first saw her; I just refused to accept that I could ever feel this way again. I was scared to accept that I had found someone I did not want to lose.

My breaths came in quick, shallow gasps as she rode me. My mind was hazed, reminiscent of the steam on the bathroom mirror, my thoughts clung to me as Cali did. Her nails dug into my back, as the thought of making Cali mine, *all mine*, gripped my head and my heart. I was captivated by her, staring into her eyes full of happiness and hope. In that instant, I craved her more than ever; I never wanted to see sadness burden those entrancing eyes of hers. I wanted to make her happy in every way possible.

My desire for her was insatiable; but this deeper attraction I had not seen coming had taken hold. I could not bear the thought of losing her, of spending a moment apart from her. Almost instantly, the cold, brutal beast I once was transformed into a soft, gentle kitten, purring contently as her inner walls engulfed my shaft. The idea that I could fill her with my seed until my heart's content, only made my growls deeper, and my hunger for her more intense.

I felt her body surrender to me. Her name rolled off my lips as I drove harder and deeper into her, the thick steam clogging my throat as I envisioned her entrance already full of my cum, recalling it trickling down her thighs from earlier. The sight of my cock coated in it as it slid in and out of her fueled my desire even more. My arms tightened around her, locking her position as close to my body as physically possible as my kisses peppered her neck frantically.

Her tears were long gone, replaced by a sparkle that danced in her eyes as they locked onto mine. "Cali" I moaned again as she rocked her hips against mine, my full length buried deep. Her arms clutched at my back, clinging to me as her muscles weakened from the multiple orgasms that rocked through her. Not once did she break eye contact, every moan, every gasp sparkled in those dark pools of hers, blinking furiously against the water that cascaded down her face. It was then that I knew she had won.

Cali was the victor of this internal battle that had been waging on in my head and my heart since meeting her. In such a short space of time, she managed to dominate my every thought, my every want, my every desire. She had ignited a hope that my future may not be as lonely and as miserable as I had once envisioned. *There is a life after Lara.*

The thought of a future with her filled me with excitement, encouraging my thrusts to quicken and plunder her warmth harder and deeper than before. She bit her lip, her forehead creased as her eyes flickered closed briefly as she succumbed to her climax. I could not hold back even if I wanted to. My seed shot forcefully inside her; pumping from my shaft in warm, numbing streams. I heard her gasp and felt her nails gouge deep grooves into my spine. I shuddered and she trembled as we came together. So normal, so natural, that I wished for this moment to never end.

I kissed her deeply as I lowered her to her feet, a satisfied grin stretched across my face while I watched my hot load leak out of her, trickling down her thighs before being washed away by the water that was now running cold from above. I turned off the water when I noticed her skin was coated in goosebumps, wrapping the towel around her and holding her body close to me. *I never want to let her go.*

"Nico," she murmured after several moments. A single tear slipped down her cheek before she leaned her forehead against mine. Her body shaking with quiet sobs instead of her orgasm. "I can't offer you a family or children. All I have to give is myself..."

My heart raced as I lifted her from the shower and carried her to the bedroom, gently laying her on the bed. I felt a sense of wonder, as my mouth explored her body, planting gentle kisses in each area, staking claim to every inch of her body.

I was lost in the moment, relishing the anticipation that swelled inside me, as I cherished the tender connection we shared. Our breaths became lighter, her body responding to each gentle caress. My thoughts lingered on my earlier revelation; She was mine, and I was hers. My head and my heart had now fully accepted this fate. There was nowhere else in the world I would have rather been, nor was there anyone else I wanted to be with.

After what seemed like an eternity of sadness and loneliness, I had finally found my happy place beside her, filling me with a contentment that I never knew was possible after Lara's death.

"Cali, *you* are all I want." I murmured against the swell of her breast, my tongue flicking across her hardened peaks, my eyes locked onto hers as my mouth drew back up to hers.

The sharp honk of a car horn jolted me awake. I stirred slowly, my head fuzzy as I tried to recollect my whereabouts. There was a pressure on my chest I was unaccustomed to. I looked down to see Cali's head resting there; the slight gentle snores tickled against the small tufts of hair that spread across it. The sight of her naked body curled next to mine evoked a warmth, a content happiness I could not ignore. I smiled, wrapping my arms around her tighter.

The horn blared a barrage of short urgent blasts which penetrated the silence. Her eyes flickered open, her eyelids too heavy, her voice nothing more than a soft whimper. "Nico? What is that noise?"

I chuckled taking in the sight of her unruly locks, each short strand flicking out in all directions. I tucked those that fell into her face behind her ears, kissing her button nose before pulling her chin closer to me. "Hello *beautiful*" I whispered, watching her cheeks flush a deep crimson before kissing her deeply. "I could get used to waking up beside you." I murmured.

Her smile crept across her face, but the moment was ruined by another blast of horns. "I'll go have a look" I said, sliding out from underneath her and strolling over to the window.

My heart dropped, my feet refused to move any closer, as I spotted the yellow cab waiting directly outside. "Nico? Who is it?" She asked, hearing her tiptoe behind me, her arms resting on my shoulders as she peered around me.

"Cali, is that your cab... waiting to take you to the airport?" I whispered, my words sticking in the back of my throat.

"Shit." She gasped, scrambling to get dressed and rushing for the door. "I knew I should have just canceled it..."

I grabbed her wrist, spinning her back into my embrace, my heart still beating slower than normal. I did not like the way my body reacted to the idea that she was leaving; it was possessive and controlling. *How am I going to let her go back to the US?* I asked myself, as her heavy, sleepy eyes stared into mine. *You're not*, the beast within growled. *She is going nowhere without us.*

"Canceled *what*?" I asked, trying to keep my voice even.

Her shoulders slumped and she bit her lip. "It was part of the honeymoon package, a complimentary couples spa retreat..." she whimpered. "I can't go there on my own..." Her eyes flickering to the cab beyond the window, her body crumpling into itself even more. "Perhaps if I ignore it...hopefully it will just leave."

I drew my hand into her hair, feeling the soft tendrils slipping through my fingers, clutching a fistful and pulling her face to mine. Relief that she was not leaving yet flooded through every fiber of my body, curling my lips into a smile.

"How about I join you?" I asked, her heart was hammering in her chest, its thrum vibrated against mine, her eyes scanned my face as if trying to find the punchline of a joke.

In the soft glow of the bedroom light overhead, her eyes shone like rich, dark chocolate, flecked with golden undertones that reflected the light. The soothing aroma of lavender lingered on her silky-smooth skin. I inhaled deeply as I buried my head into her neck, my lips finding the base of it, planting delicate, feather-light kisses. *She is beautiful* I thought as my arms drew around her, the creature within me stirred, sleepily adding *and I never want to be without her.*

"Really?" she asked, her words flickered across my lips, feeling her tremble with anticipation. I held her for a few more seconds, inhaling her scent; the mixture of vanilla and lavender mixed with the lingering aroma of our sex.

My kisses slowly gravitated down her neck, "uh-huh" I purred, feeling her pulse quicken beneath my touch. "Of course," I whispered, "I would go anywhere with you, *Thea.*" My hand slowly threading deeper into the silky tendrils of her mahogany hair. "*Thea*, I will do anything for you." I whispered as I pulled away from her to see her reaction. My own heart thumping in my ears seeing her smile, noticing two small dimples indented in her flushed cheeks. Another blast of the car horn shattered the tranquility of our closeness, "though I suppose we should hurry." I chuckled reluctantly letting her hair fall out of my grasp.

"Thank you, Nico" she purred, her hands sliding down the sides of my body, lingering just above my hips. "Thank you for everything."

In the backseat of the taxi, a comfortable silence enveloped us. Her head gently rested on my shoulder and our fingers intertwined as they rested on my thigh. It had been such a long time that anyone's fingers had filled the gaps between mine, yet ours had found each other with minds of their own, slotting together like pieces of a puzzle.

For years I had been lost, cast adrift by the ravaging storm of sorrow and misery, my life washed in gray, deary hues. Andreas had called her *"ray of sunshine,"* and that was exactly what she was. From the moment she had entered my life, her radiance had slowly broken through the clouds, her light and warmth filtered through them, bringing the vibrant colors back into my life.

An icy shiver shuddered through my body as Lara's voice whispered through the crack of the window, *"What about me, Nico?"* Her words dripped with jealousy and loathing. I quickly wound up the window, shutting her out. *Lara, I'm sorry, but I must move on...*

I leaned down and pressed my lips against the crown of Cali's head, inhaling the soothing scent of lavender that clung to her hair and skin, embracing the gentle thrum of my heartbeat at her closeness.

"Cute couple," the cab driver remarked, his green eyes glancing at us through the rear-view mirror. "The gods must have smiled upon you at your wedding." I noticed Cali's lips parting to respond, but I gently traced my thumb over her soft, plump lips, diverting her attention.

"There are worse things he could think than us being married," I whispered in her ear, watching as a shy smile spread across her face, her cheeks flushing with warmth. "He could have thought I was your father."

She swatted me playfully, her eyes glinting with happiness and her smile widened. "You are not *that* much older than me." she smirked. The cab driver had started a conversation with Cali but my mind had wandered to an image of Cali gliding toward me in a delicate lace wedding dress, an altar placed on the beach with a small handful of faceless people on either side of the aisle. Tropical flowers in full bloom in the bouquet she carried; a multitude of yellows almost as bright as the radiant smile that was spreading across her face as she approached.

"Nico..." Cali's voice jolted me from the daydream, her eyes studying my face, "what were you thinking about?" She asked. "I have never seen you smile like that before." I pulled her closer to me, as a bittersweet taste flooded my mouth; had she not discovered Adam's infidelity, she would not be here with me but with *him* instead. I knew how much his betrayal had hurt her, how it had knocked her confidence and her trust in others. Yet, without the pain she had suffered, nothing between us would have ever blossomed. Andreas' wise words filtered into my thoughts resonating deep in my chest. *Sometimes we need darkness to show us the light and sometimes we need to experience pain to show us the path to our true happiness.*

"You, Cali... I was thinking of you." Her blush deepened as I stared into her eyes. *I am falling fast for you Cali. I am imagining a future with you.* Lara's face flitted into my mind, her sorrowful eyes piercing my soul, her arms outstretched with her skeletal fingers trying to grasp me, to hold onto me. A shiver ran along my spine as I tried to block the image out.

With an abrupt screech of tires on the dry asphalt, the cab came to a halt. Outside, a grand stone building loomed, its tall arches framing stained glass windows. A set of impressive giant oak doors, intricately carved with swirls and small flowers.

As we approached the entrance a woman with sleek black hair neatly twisted into a clip greeted us. "Sir, you will go that way; ma'am, please follow me." Her voice was gentle yet authoritative, and I could feel her noticing my hesitation to release Cali's hand.

"You two lovebirds will be spending the entire afternoon together," she assured us with a smile. "I promise."

As we were guided into the individual changing rooms, I stared at Cali, her eyes open in awe as she took in the surroundings. This was a very elite and prestigious spa resort; a place Lara had begged me to take her but we had never gotten around to it. Known for its celebrity clientele and high-end boutique products, this place oozed with luxurious comfort. The air was thick with a variety of calming scents from eucalyptus oils to honey and flora. It instantly soothed and coaxed an inner peace.

Cali's eyes caught mine from across the room, stopping just before she disappeared behind a heavy velvet curtain that covered the ladies' changing rooms. I recognized that look; Lara had shown it thousands of times over the years; a longing that penetrated deep into her soul. A look of unshielded love. I gave her a smile, trying to return the look despite the ominous presence of Lara lurching over my shoulder.

I was ushered quickly into the changing rooms, where I ditched all of my belongings into a locker made of dark oak, and tore off my clothes. I had not been prepared for a visit here, most would adorn their swimwear, but as I looked at myself in the full-length mirror, all I had was my thin black boxers. They left little to the imagination, the outline of my flaccid cock pressed against my thigh. I slipped on the white robe and tightened it around my waist. I thought of Cali's delicious body, slipping into her bikini. The silky olive skin that my tongue has traced a multitude of times these past few days.

My cock stirred, hardening at the thought of her. *Fuck.* I tightened the robe a little bit more, hoping the excess material would disguise my arousal. Slipping my feet into the white slippers I had been issued, they clicked along the ceramic tiles as I was led down a narrow hallway. A billow of steam escaped the door as it was held open for me.

"She is waiting for you." The husky tones of my escort said. He was not native to this country, his dark complexion and heavy African accent gave it away, but his Greek was fluent. I nodded, stepping into the sauna, immediately embraced by the comforting warmth of eucalyptus-enthused steam.

True to his words, I found myself reunited with Cali when she stepped into the sauna. The air was thick with heat and steam, obscuring everything but her silhouette as she moved closer. "Nico," she breathed, reaching out for me until her fingers connected with mine.

The puzzle was complete. Alone in the sauna, just Cali and me, the rest of the world disappeared behind the heavy fog that hung in the air. "Cali..." I purred, pulling her towards me. My hands instinctively slipped under her robe as I embraced her.

My fingers swirled against her skin, trailing down her spine, lingering on the small of her back. My fingertips expecting to brush against the waistline of her bikini bottoms. They stilled as they traced the area where it should have been while my cock protested against my boxers.

"I think you forgot something," I whispered. My hands trailed along her hips down to the curve of her ass feeling the soft bare skin beneath my touch and feeling her squirm at the slightest movement.

"I... um... we- we left in such a hurry." she stuttered, I could detect the embarrassed tone in her voice. An involuntary growl resonated through my chest as my hands grabbed her bare buttocks tight in my palms holding her against me. My rigid cock threatened to burst through the flimsy fabric of my underwear at any moment. Her breaths quickened as she drew her arms around my neck pressing her body against it.

The dim lighting inside the sauna cast everything but her into dark shadows, soft music vibrated through every molecule of the rising steam creating a thrum of palpable intimacy. We lingered in the moment breathing in the rich scent of eucalyptus. I could feel everything clicking into place; everything finally making sense.

My longing for her began to consume me, guiding my hands along her thighs and up to her unshielded slit. She gasped as my fingers explored her warmth, her body yielding to my touch, lifting her leg up onto the nearest bench. An invitation for them to venture deeper.

The surrounding darkness had become our cocoon of intimacy, relaxing our bodies and our minds so we could act on our deepest desire. Her hand snaked its way beneath my boxers gliding over it with the lightest touch. She cupped my balls, before sliding her hand back along my full, erect length. I wanted her, in this sensual environment, more than I had ever wanted anyone.

Suddenly her other hand was placed on my chest, slowly guiding me to the bench. I watched as her silhouette shrunk to the floor and freed my shaft from its confines. Her breath was hot against it as her lips enveloped the tip. Feeling the hot air escape her nostrils against my groin as her tongue teased every nerve ending of my engorged and throbbing head.

I pushed my hips forward, my body tingling with anticipation as her lips enveloped me. Inch by inch, her warm, wet mouth descended with a tantalizing slowness that drove me wild. Her gaze met mine, barely visible among the thick steam, the hint of a smile played on her lips against my cock as she moved along it stoking the inferno inside me even more.

Just as I felt the pressure building, she let her robe slip away, the soft fabric pooling around my feet. The outline of her form bent before me, devouring my shaft with a frivolous passion left me breathless and eager for more.

Twenty

Cali

Nico's engorged tip throbbed against my tongue as my mouth wrapped around him, his soft moans of pleasure encouraged me to proceed. The scent of him as his pre-cum dribbled against my tongue hung heavier in my nostrils than the aroma of eucalyptus that hung in the dense steam that encompassed the two of us.

I squirmed as he clutched a fistful of my hair, using it to guide my head up and down his length, setting the rhythm that made his shaft twitch beneath my lips. I hollowed my cheeks, enjoying the grunts that vibrated through his whole body. My nose pressed against the base of his length, gagging as his head tickled my tonsils. I welcomed him deeper, feeling it glide along the back of my throat.

The air was thick. Nico's hands held my head firm in place, lodging his shaft so deep in my throat it made breathing difficult. I almost choked as his seed exploded, hitting my tonsils before slipping down my throat. I gulped and swallowed every drop, ignoring the fire in my lungs and the dizzying sensation in my head.

"Cali... fuck..." he groaned, releasing his tight grasp on my hair and sliding his cock out of my mouth. His breathing was hard, ragged as if he had just run a marathon. I gripped onto his thighs as I gasped for breath.

His lips enveloped mine, his hands guiding my core down onto his shaft, feeling my warmth yield to him easily.

"Nico" I sighed as I ground my hips against him. "I'm scared to get hurt again." I whimpered, my fingers teasing a tendril of his hair. "I couldn't give Adam- I can't-" A tear slid down my cheek, his finger was quick to catch it and wipe it away. "I'm scared that I am not enough for you."

My chest tightened as I felt my sobs trying to break free. His hands moved to the side of my head, holding it firmly so that I could see into his eyes. "Cali, you are *more* than enough." His voice asserted calmly, continuing his hard thrusts into my core, never once breaking eye contact.

"Fuck him" Nico muttered. "Adam took you for granted and now he has lost you... *to me*." He thrust his shaft even deeper with slow precise movements. We were no longer fucking to get our urgent release, allowing it to slowly build relishing this sensual moment. It dawned on me that this was what it felt like to make love to the true Nico Karamanlis, a man who was no longer afraid to show his emotions to me.

"Cali, I will never hurt you -"

"Shh" I whispered, my lips pressing against his, silencing him. I did not need to hear the words to know that Nico would never treat me the way Adam did. My lips pulled into a small smile, thankful that I had found someone who would cherish me and love me, despite how little we knew of each other, I knew that what we shared was real.

I was free-falling once more, hard and fast in this whirlwind romance I had never seen coming. Nico deepened every tender kiss he sprung upon my lips as together we rode the blissful waves of our orgasm, while our hearts and our moans fell into perfect synchrony.

I realized that I had been living in fear, that I had allowed my insecurities to consume me, but Nico made me want to confront these demons, his sensual touch and his heartfelt words gave me a glimmer of hope that we could have a future together.

The weight of my insecurities lifted off my shoulders, I could breathe easy, as Nico's kisses fluttered across my lips. My body and my soul had succumbed completely to him, the sensuality of that moment had brought us together closer than I could have ever imagined.

Twenty-One

Nico

"Cali... I don't want you to leave."

Cali's hips suddenly stilled and every muscle in her body tensed. Her arms that were draped around my neck felt heavy like planks of wood, rigid and solid.

Time seemed to stretch endlessly in the silence that followed. Only our ragged breaths could be heard. Anxiety loomed over me like a dark shadow, the ominous feeling of loneliness and the anticipation of heartbreak. I was sure Cali could hear my heart as it pounded loudly in my chest. The rhythm echoed the powerful barrage of intense drums found in a heavy metal track.

I found myself on the edge of emotional breakdown, where my hopes and fears twisted together like the strands of a tightly woven rope. Through the thick haze, I could see the conflict surfacing behind her eyes as she considered her options.

"I have to go back," she whispered. "My mom..."

"I'll come with you," I blurted out, my heart frantic, goosebumps prickled and my chest tightened at the thought of her leaving. "Cali... I *want* to come with you."

"Nico, you can't do that," she replied, "I couldn't expect you to drop all your responsibilities you have here *for me.*"

"Cali, *none* of that matters-" She broke away from me, suddenly rising to her feet with a heavy sigh.

Without her warmth, my body ached, leaving me adrift in the thick steam. I felt the eucalyptus choke me, the fog clogging the back of my throat. She took several steps back until her features blurred into a faceless shadow.

"My flight is tomorrow," she said softly. "I need to go home, Nico, and you need to stay here."

"Is this about Adam... *Cali*, do you still have feelings for him?" I asked, my voice barely above a whisper.

I watched her almost shapeless form shake its head and put on the robe once more before fading further into the fog, leaving behind just a delicate trace of her existence. It was an unspoken warning - I was losing her.

"No, Nico, not anymore. You made me realize that... but what about *her*, Nico? Are you truly ready to let go of Lara... to move on?"

An icy grip strangled me, compressing the air in my lungs as if caught in an unyielding vice as Lara's ghostly apparition materialized in the gap between Cali and me.

The air around us froze, as Lara's black soulless eyes penetrated the thick fog and locked onto mine. Her gaunt, unnatural lips twisted into a sinister grin and her lifeless hair hung down, dripping water until it formed a puddle beneath her skeletal feet. She advanced toward me in slow, gradual steps with her hands extended in my direction.

I tried to move closer to Cali's shadow, I wanted her to see me confront Lara's ghost once and for all; to see that I was ready to move on - I was ready to give myself completely to Cali. It was crucial for her to recognize the sincerity in my gaze.

I tried to side step Lara, to ignore her presence completely. "All I want is to make you happy, to be with you... to *love* you... I am ready to move on with my life... a life with you in it."

I noticed Lara's expression change as her icy fingers clutched my arms. Her anguish that had marked her downcast features began to fade as a radiant glow surrounded her. "Nico?" Lara asked softly. "You will never see me again."

I held my breath and nodded, squinting my eyes as Lara's features slowly returned to the woman who I had once loved, looking as beautiful as the day I last saw her all those years ago. Her blonde curls cascaded down the shoulders of her black lace dress, and her eyes returned to their brilliant pools of oceanic blue that pierced my soul. She smiled. "Nico, I want you to be happy," she murmured. "Even if that is without me."

Almost immediately the palpable tension in the room eased as the weight that crushed my chest east. I felt like an albatross in flight, free and unburdened, soaring above the waves of my grief and heartache. In the blink of an eye, Lara disappeared, taking with her the constricting pressure from my chest. I took a deep breath; my heart was my own once more - mine to give to Cali unconditionally.

With the resurgence of vibrancy in my life, I found myself searching for Cali among the thick steam. I wanted to wrap her in my tender embrace and comfort her; to reassure her that although Lara will forever hold a special place in my memories, I was ready for a future with Cali.

My gaze swept through the mist, desperately seeking her out. I turned full circle expecting to see her lurking in the darkest of shadows waiting for me - but I was alone. Cali was gone.

Twenty-Two

***Cali** - twelve hours later.*

I was slowly drowning in the sea of faces, unable to catch my breath as the bodies crashed against me in every direction. The piercing glare of artificial lights assaulted my tired eyes as soon as I stepped inside the airport, and the sudden thrum of energy pulsated in my temples. I had not missed the chaos of the US, even in the early hours of the morning the airport was teeming with life. It made me feel more isolated and alone among the thrum of people going about their lives. All of them unhindered and unaware of the pain I was suffering inside.

I navigated my way through the claustrophobic throng of people, faceless blurs on either side of me. I missed the tranquility and calm of the ocean; its gentle hiss as the waves lapped against the soft white shore with the distant symphony of cicadas in the background. I felt lost; a stranger cast adrift in unfamiliar land. *This is not my home.*

A sharp ache filled the Nico-shaped void in my heart as the truth crushed me like a heavy weight. *My true home is with Nico Karamanlis.*

It was surreal how our attraction had started off as pure unadulterated lust that quickly blossomed into a deeper connection. Almost as if our relationship were scripted from the pages of a romance novel, one not too dissimilar to the one I had been reading to my mom prior to my departure to Rhodes.

I did not want to leave him, but I knew I had to. I had fought against the gravitational pull of his charm from the very moment I had walked out of the sauna. My guilt had gnawed at my insides like a rabid animal, still chewing away at them now as I stood in the arrival lobby.

Yet, as I found myself wandering through the security gates, a tidal wave of emotions overcame me that left me breathless and disorientated. Nico's words echoed in my ears and reverberated in my chest as I closed the door of the sauna behind me. *"Cali... I love you."*

Still, no matter how much the connection meant to either of us, the truth that perhaps we did truly love each other, there was no chance of true happiness while the lingering presence of his deceased wife and daughter cast shadows over him. I could not be sure that he was genuinely ready to let them go. *Or is that just my excuse to run, because I am terrified of being hurt once again?*

"Cali?" A female voice cut through my reverie, pulling me back to the present. It was the last person I expected, or wanted, to see - Stephanie. It was clear in her tired expression that she had been waiting a while for me to arrive. Her gaze faltered as her guilt-stricken conscience was exposed.

It was obvious she had come to seek my forgiveness, her hope that I could forget all the wrongs she had done to me. She was mistaken, I was not capable of granting her such generosity.

Stephanie's eyes were swollen and red, but what was more noticeable was the distinctive swell of her abdomen. Despite her best efforts to conceal it beneath a loose jumper and slouching in her seat, it was as obvious. This pregnancy was not new, not recent, she had been concealing it from me for quite some time. Her gaze followed mine as she stood up to meet me.

I noticed that as she walked towards me her gait had developed into a waddle, one that only those in the late stages of pregnancy developed. My stomach churned as her arms cradled her stomach protectively as she came to a stop a few feet from me. My shoulders crumpled at the sight of her and at the realization that their sordid tryst had been going on for a lot longer than I had feared.

My breath slipped away from me like air from a punctured balloon, gasping out from my lungs as I withered, surrendering to the suffocating grip of hatred. I struggled to keep my tears in check while bile rose in the back of my throat. Stephanie was everything I could never be - a mother.

Suddenly, her gaze shot up, and the intensity of her emotions, combined with the glow radiating from her skin sucked the air from my lungs. At that moment, I realized that no matter how hard I tried, regardless of no longer wanting to be with Adam; forgiveness would never come.

Everything Stephanie and I had been through in the past felt irrelevant now. All those times I cried to her when my period came, another failed attempt to conceive. Every time she reassured me that Adam and I did not need children to have a happy and fulfilled life. Every word of comfort she gave me when I told her we were going through IVF treatment. All of it meant nothing as she stood bearing Adam's child before me.

The foundation of our friendship was built on trust, on love for each other's happiness. She may as well have been wielding a sledgehammer in her hands, as our friendship lay smashed to smithereens. She had destroyed everything the moment she opened her legs for my fiancé and sought solace in his arms.

"Cali..." she cried, her whole body shaking as she sobbed. "I'm so sorry, please—" I raised my hand to stop her. My gaze was locked firmly on her swollen stomach. It had stricken me like a kick to my empty ovaries, the depth of their deception, the extent of their lies. *They were both playing me for a fool all along.*

"What are you doing here, Steph?" I asked, my voice thick with hatred that made Stephanie recoil and flinch. She wrapped her arms tighter around her midriff, biting on her lower lip trying to suppress her sobs.

"Adam mentioned your return flight... he doesn't know I'm here." She stuttered, tears clung to her eyelashes as she looked at me. "I know he visited you; he said he wanted to tell you in person—"

"You shouldn't have come, Steph." I interrupted harshly. "I will never forgive you. Not only did you betray me... but you are having his child." I hissed.

"It wasn't— I never— Cali, I can't lose you; you're my best friend—"

"*Was.*" I cut her off, my eyes icy. Her sobs erupted into loud cries. I could feel the weight of stares on us, witnessing the moment I made a pregnant woman wail in public. My hands balled into fits, my nails biting into the fleshy palms like tiny knives.

"How long have you and Adam been fucking behind my back?" I glanced down to her stomach once again. "And please do tell me the truth for once"

She couldn't meet my gaze, her shoulders trembling with each sob. "Almost a year," she finally murmured. "It started as a foolish, drunken mistake... after Carl and I broke up..."

I had tuned out completely, the rising tide of nausea churning violently in my stomach as I leaned over the nearest trash can to heave. She reached out to console me, but I pushed her away in frustration. "A *fucking* year?" I spat, wiping at my mouth with the sleeve of my cardigan. "You and Adam... a *fucking year!*"

Her sobs grew louder, my name ricocheted off every surface of the lobby, but I continued to walk away from her. My stomach twisted; I knew I should no longer care; Adam meant nothing to me now; neither of them did.

White hot tears streamed down my face; my face flushed from the stares passers-by were giving me. There were only two people I wanted to see - who could make me feel better. Yet only one of them was in this country: my mom.

I hailed a cab, ignoring Steph's voice that was growing closer behind me. "To the hospital." I barked slamming the door. The cab driver looked in his rearview mirror, a quizzical look on his face.

"Am I waiting for her?" He asked, I shook my head as I twisted in my seat catching a glimpse of Stephanie frantically waving and calling my name.

"No."

The cab driver fell into silence as he pulled out of the bay, his eyes flickered to me every now and then. His lips were pursed as if wanting to say something, but the cold look I flashed back at him kept him quiet.

I fought back the nausea that clogged my throat and churned my stomach as the conversation with Stephanie replayed in my mind. *"Almost a year..."* Vivid images of their betrayal invaded my thoughts; I should have noticed something was off when she chose a shapeless maid of honor dress over the one she had originally loved. A sleek, silky number that hugged her flawless and slim figure.

I recalled the extra pounds she had put on, in all the years I had known Stephanie, she was always conscious of her weight and her figure. She looked almost unhealthy to me, and seeing her with a little bit more weight on her had pleased me. It had eased my mind that she was slowly accepting the advice I had been giving her for years.

The cab drew to a slow stop outside the hospital entrance; his hand outstretched waiting for payment. *Shit.* "Do you take card payments?" I asked, frantically digging in my purse for notes that were not Euros. Thankfully he nodded, muttering under his breath about an additional charge. I was no longer paying attention, guilt had struck knowing that I had neglected my mother in the past few weeks, I had not even called her. *I was too caught up with Nico to care.*

I gulped as the machine beeped loudly, grateful that there were sufficient funds in the account to cover the fare before fleeing the cab without a moment to waste.

The sterile reception area was eerily quiet, the receptionist busy typing away on the computer in front of her, a phone tucked between her ear and neck. She recognized me, from my countless visits, her gaze held me in place. I could tell something was wrong.

"I have been trying to call you, Cali." Her voice was soft, "she has deteriorated quickly in the last twelve hours..."

I sprinted towards her ward; I had learned these hallways like the back of my hand. My nostrils were familiar to the sharp scent of disinfectant as I flew through the maze of corridors. I had been oblivious to the various beeping machines from the other patients, but as I turned the corner, the looming dread of death gripped me as the monotonous beep grew louder.

The sight of doctors and nurses swarmed around my mother's bed sent a chill down my spine. I quickened my steps, my heart pounding with each one. "Mom!" I called out, my voice shrill and panicked. I was standing in the doorframe when strong hands held me back, preventing me from moving closer to her.

"No!" I cried, tears streaming down my face, my eyes glancing to the many machines connected to my mother with thin transparent tubes. The crowd around her shifted, giving me a fleeting view of her still form. Her skin was deathly pale, her lips were blue and her hand hung limply over the side of the bed.

Suddenly, her body jolted upright as the defibrillator delivered its electric shock. Once, twice, and then a third time. Each jolt felt like a dagger to my heart. The continuous beep of the ECG machine echoed my deepest dread. *I am too late. My mother is gone.*

"I'm sorry" the nurse whispered as he loosened his grip on my arms. His eyes studied me from behind his round spectacles, his mouth pulled into a tight line. I tried to look around his solid mass, blocking her from my view.

"Time of death: ten-eleven am." The doctor's voice from inside my mother's room chanted. I felt the floor give way; the male nurse too slow to catch me as I crumpled to a heap. Every tear and sob I had suppressed from landing in the US erupted like a burst fire hydrant.

"We will get her prepped for you to see her." The male nurse said, his arms lifting me to my feet, maneuvering me away from her room to some seats further down the hall. My legs felt like lumps of lead, disconnected from my body; each stride heavy and cumbersome. I slumped in the seat, unable to stop my sobs as what felt like an eternity passed until I was allowed into her room.

I grasped her hands; still slightly warm beneath my fingertips despite their ghostly white color. *I should have been here. I should never have left.*

My cries tore through me as my guilt and regret manifested within me; snaking its way around my body, constricting every muscle and forcing the air from my lungs. I had missed my chance to say goodbye. I had allowed my selfishness to consume me. I had let her suffer alone. *I was all she had and I had abandoned her.*

Adam's words reverberated in my head, *"Once your mother dies, you will have nothing. No one."* As much as I hated to admit it, he was right. There was nothing for me here, no job, no home, no future.

The clock's relentless ticking filled the silence as I sat next to her. My body trembled as deep, wrenching sobs broke free. All the sorrow and anguish I had bottled up inside now exploded fiercely. The burden of my grief was overwhelming, and I sank beside her, clutching her hand tightly. The weight of it was immense. It dawned on me then, *perhaps I had been too harsh on Nico. How must he feel to have grieved his wife and his young child? How could I expect him to move on so easily when he saw his entire life and future destroyed before his very eyes?*

The abruptness of his wife and child's death was a heartbreak I could not even imagine experiencing. At least I had time to prepare myself for this, my mother's battle with cancer had been a long and grueling experience. I had known it was coming.

There was nothing Nico could have done to prepare himself for his loss, so sudden and unexpected, it was no wonder why he struggled to let them go. The knots in my stomach tightened, I had expected too much from Nico. I had placed unrealistic expectations on him; I could have been more compassionate towards his struggles. I should have reached out to support him with his healing, so he would not have to face it alone. *I should have shown him that I could help him move on.*

His face flashed in my mind, the sun-kissed glow of his skin, while his creamy caramel eyes held the depth of his sorrow, like a mirror reflecting the pain of losing his family that lingered like an open wound. *Would he ever find it in his heart to forgive me?*

My heart ached as a deep longing rippled through my body, a homesickness that I could not soothe. What I wanted, *needed* now, was hundreds of miles away. *Would Nico still embrace me with the same warmth as before?*

The white sterile walls seemed to close in around me, the slatted blinds on the windows let in the monotonous hue from the gloomy weather outside. All color faded from my world. Both of my hands enveloped my mother's, bringing it to my lips as I muttered endless apologies in my hope that her soul was still listening. Praying that she could forgive me for not being with her.

After what felt like an eternity, crying until I had run out of tears, I was quietly led out of her room and into the quiet refuge of the hospital chapel. The male nurse had whispered more condolences as he handed me a small bag containing the meager personal belongings my mother had with her. I glanced at them briefly before taking a few steps into the chapel.

The walls had been painted a deep burgundy, as matching heavy velvet drapes blocked all natural light from filtering into the room. There was a welcoming comfort that emanated from the candles that were lit on either side of the room. A rich fragrance of incense and candle wax soothed my palette from the sterile chemicals used throughout the rest of the hospital. For a moment, I almost forgot where I was.

As I made my way down the narrow aisle lined with wooden benches, my gaze swept over the room, evoking memories of the aisle I had missed on my wedding day. My knuckles turned pale as I gripped a brown paper bag filled with my mom's few possessions, while my small suitcase trailed behind me. My breath clogged my throat as it dawned on me that the contents of these were all that I had to my name.

I settled into the bench closest to the imposing oak crucifix that adorned the wall at the front of the chapel. The wood groaned softly under my weight as I sank into it. I picked through the contents of the brown paper bag; her watch and some jewelry along with her tatty leather purse that she had used for as long as I can remember. My fingertips brushed the cool glass of her iPhone at the bottom of the bag. I smiled as I retrieved it, fondly remembering the day I gifted it to her, the day after the hospital staff had warned me that she would not be leaving the hospital.

She had struggled to use it, so different from her old phone with large, easy-to-see buttons, she had not been able to navigate this newer model with a touchscreen and facial recognition. It had taken several weeks to adapt, and with the help of nursing staff she was soon video calling me every night and sending me silly videos she found on the internet during the day when she was bored and I was not beside her.

I unlocked it with her access code and scrolled through our steady stream of messages. A pang of sadness flooded my heart when I saw she had tried to call and message my phone, which was now smashed to pieces and dumped in a landfill somewhere. That was when I saw she had been in contact with Andreas, the same time every evening without fail since my arrival in Rhodes. My heart paused momentarily when I realized he was the last person she had spoken to; his text message explaining that I was on my way home. *Nico must have told him.*

With trembling fingers I hit the call button beside his name, holding my breath while the shrill ringing sound came from the line, almost drowned out by my pulse that throbbed in my ears.

"Hello?" A groggy voice, thick with sleep, answered on the other end.

"Andreas?" My voice trembled. "Andreas... My mother..." Sobs wracked my body as he fell silent. "She's gone." I heard him whimper on the other end of the phone, the two of us unspeaking as we cried together.

Tears streamed down my cheeks as I stared at the crumpled piece of paper clenched tightly in my shaking hands. I held my breath as I remembered the night he had left it on my bedside cabinet. The frantic and rushed way he had scrawled his number on it in his slanted handwriting. This was the only thing I had left of him, aside from my memories.

I need you, I typed to the one person who could truly grasp my grief. *Nico, I'm so sorry...*

Twenty-Three

***Cali** - three weeks later.*

I never received a reply. It had been a few weeks since I had sent the message, three weeks exactly since my mother had passed, but Nico had not even read the message. It hurt more knowing that Nico was choosing to ignore me than anything else right now.

The rest of my mind and body was numb. I had made all of the preparations alone, desensitized and disconnected as if it were for a stranger rather than my own mother. The preparations had not taken as long as I had feared; though everything was held up while I had waited for her life insurance to pay out her already paid-for funeral care plan to cover the costs of her burial.

Every single day, my thoughts drifted to him. Seeing his caramel eyes light up with joy when he smiled, and recalling the comforting warmth of his strong arms wrapped around me. I wished he was here. I wish I had taken him up on his offer to come with me.

The cold, dreary weather beyond the motel's window made me snuggle deeper into the duvet. I was not ready to face the world alone. The moment I was released from the hospital hours after her passing, this motel immediately came to mind. I found myself without a place to go; my mother's house had been sold to settle her medical bills, and returning to the home I once shared with Adam was out of the question.

Each day, as I made my way to my mother's bedside, I drove past this motel. It resembled any typical establishment, once boasting a modern and sleek design with an abundance of metal and glass, all sharp angles and clean lines. However, now it appeared worn and weary, tired and barely standing.

Several windows were boarded up and spots of thick red rust blemished the once shiny chrome finish. The rates were affordable, and I managed to snag a discount for paying for the month in advance, but that nearly depleted the last of my funds.

A wave of anxiety washed over me; I had procrastinated long enough. I needed to embark on the daunting task of finding a new job to make ends meet. Considering I had stepped away from my previous position to support my mother through her illness, my finances were drained. Although I was set to inherit some money, I could not help but wonder if, after covering her final medical bills and funeral costs, there would be anything left for me at all.

I checked flights to Rhodes daily, contemplating splurging the last of my funds in the hope of surprising him after her funeral, but every time I went to book one I found myself backing out. *I am not ready to face his rejection.*

Cocooned in bed, I pulled out my mom's cell, scrolling through her messages, seeking comfort in the short but loving exchanges between her and Andreas. I longed to message, to ask how Nico was, but I never did. I would type the message, my thumb would hover over the send button with an aching heart, but then I would delete it.

I wished I could forget about it all, about my feelings for him, about Adam and Stephanie. I had no more tears left to cry, my heart was shattered into a million pieces and the nausea was still lurking in the pit of my stomach.

My muscles screamed as I dragged myself to the bathroom, only just reaching the toilet before vomiting. My breath caught in my throat, my body felt heavier, fuller. *Nico needs to know.*

I should have been excited, ecstatic even, but I could not revel in the news. My pulse raced, unsure how he would react, or whether he would even talk to me, but either way he had just as much right to know as I did.

I hit the call button on Andreas' number, holding my breath. After five rings he answered, he could not hide the surprise in his voice. "Cali?"

My cries broke free, turning me into a complete wreck, my words tumbling out in a jumbled mess as he struggled to make sense of them. "Cali, let me get Nico," he said abruptly.

His soothing voice was like a balm to my ears, even though it carried a sense of urgency. "Hello? Cali?"

Tears streamed down my face once more. "Nico, you- I-" My body shook with sobs, and my breath came in quick gasps. My hands were clammy, and I nearly dropped the phone.

"Cali, what's going on?"

"Nico, I'm so sorry. I don't know if Andreas mentioned my mother... I didn't want to leave... I'm truly sorry, Nico, and I completely understand if you never want to talk to me again... but there's something you need to know."

The line fell silent for a moment. "Cali, please, just tell me what's wrong." His voice was genuine, gentle, and filled with concern. "Let me know how I can help, what do you need from me?"

"I need you..." I whispered, biting my bottom lip to try and steady my breathing as they came in rapid and shallow gasps. "Nico... I never thought it was possible, but...I'm pregnant."

Twenty-Four

Nico

Sandcastles. The ones she made, had lasted almost three days before succumbing to the Grecian tide. They had lasted almost as long as we had, though she would forever have a lasting imprint in my memory and in my heart.

Out of my apartment window I had watched the day bleed into night then back into day as I thought about her. The soft, silky olive skin, her dark cocoa eyes, those plump and juicy lips. I recalled her smile, her laughter, her moans of pleasure. *I miss her.*

The ghosts of Lara and Eve were gone, I had finally been able to let them go, to be at peace in the afterlife. I knew I would never stop loving them, but Cali had ignited a fire within that had thawed my frozen heart. Her absence had created a void that I was not able to ignore.

For days, I wallowed in self-pity, neglecting my responsibility to run Aphrodite's, strolling through the streets of Greece in the hope of catching a glimpse of her smile as memories of our short time together flooded over me like tidal waves.

I regretted not jumping in a cab and going straight to the airport, if not to stop her, to join her. Instead, by the time I had made it to the main entrance of the spa, the cab was nothing more than a yellow dot in the distance.

Does she think about me as I think of her?

I snatched up my phone for the first time in days, kicking myself as I realized the battery had died. I sat impatiently as it charged enough to flicker to life, my screen pinged with several missed calls and messages, all from Andreas, apart from one. It was from Cali, over two weeks ago. *Has it really been that long?* I asked myself as I opened the message.

I need you. Nico, I'm sorry.

I didn't waste a second, I tried to call her but it just rang until it reached voicemail. *Do I leave a message?* I shook my head and stowed my phone in my pocket as I went about my usual routine. My heart hammering in my chest, my head drafting up plans so that I could go to her.

I have found something worth fighting for, something I wanted to live for, but the US was a big place, how would I find her? What about the bar-

"Nico, aderfos mou, *my brother*. Where have you been?" Andreas called as he jogged towards me, his pale blue eyes pierced mine. "Cali... she is on the phone!"

My heart leapt as I snatched the phone from his outstretched hand. His tired eyes were watery, his hands were shaking as he relinquished his grip. "She is very upset, Nico." he sighed, "I could not make sense of what was wrong, but it is something big."

"Hello? Cali?" I asked, greeted by a chorus of heart-breaking sobs. For weeks, I had longed to hear her voice, but nothing had prepared me to hear her sobs. Listening to her apologize for leaving, hearing the regret and pain sour her voice.

"Cali, please, just tell me what's wrong." I gasped, my concern seeping through my voice, my heart gripped my icy tendrils as I waited for her response.

"Nico... I need you" her voice was almost inaudible, as the grip on my chest tightened. *I need you too,* I longed to tell her, but since her abrupt departure I had become an empty, hollow shell. I had regressed back into old habits, armoring myself, not wanting to feel this pain any more. But I could not bring myself to touch another woman, I did not want to be with anyone except Cali.

"Nico... I never thought it was possible, but...I'm pregnant."

The room started to spin, my heart was pounding, sweat beaded my forehead. "Cali, is this true?" I whimpered, my bottom lip quivering.

"Yes," she sighed, her words filtering through the breaks in her sobs. "I did multiple tests...when my period was late... they all came back positive... it's still early stages but... Nico, I don't know how I should feel..."

"Cali, I have to ask... is it mine?" I gulped, my pulse quickened.

"Yes Nico, I have only been with you." she paused. "I only want to be with you."

A smile crept onto my face - my thoughts became clear. I wanted her, and I wanted our child too. "I love you" I suddenly blurted, surprising us both. My heart raced as I waited for her response. I didn't have to wait long.

"I love you too!" she cried.

"Cali, where are you?"

Her words tumbled too fast, but I caught important snippets. "Nico, I'm sorry if this is not what you want..."

I paused, gasping for breath. "Cali, I want you, I was us... I want *our* child."

Her sobs tugged at my heartstrings, I hated to hear her cry, "Cali, I am coming for you... I will get the next flight available."

She sniffed, "Thank you Nico, my mom's funeral is soon...I have never felt so alone."

Her words hit me like a punch to the stomach. "Cali, you will not be alone for much longer. I will be there. I swear on my life, nothing will stop me getting to you."

I hung up the phone and ran through the bar to seek Andreas. I wrapped my arms around him, and let my sobs escape once and for all. Allowing every emotion to fill me and escape through my tears. "Andreas... Cali is pregnant..."

My hands were trembling as I stepped out of the cab, checking my pockets that I had everything. I was a mess; anxiety and excitement pulsed through me as I eyed the chaotic atmosphere, the throngs of people migrating into the departures section of the airport. Fear and adrenaline coursed through my veins; I had never flown before, and after the incident I had never wanted to step foot off the island ever. Yet here I was, willing to travel hundreds, *thousands*, of miles across the great open ocean that had claimed the lives of my wife and daughter for *her. Cali.*

The mere thought of her soothed me, the knowledge that in several hours I would see her smiling face, those gorgeous eyes of melted cocoa. I would be able to kiss those plump lips once more and hold her in my arms. *When I get to her, I am never letting her go.*

I took a deep breath as I stepped inside the airport. Instantly, I was engulfed by a sea of people, slowly drowning in the chaotic noises and blinded by the artificial lights. Everyone here was in a hurry; most were tourists with faces resembling a mixture of remorse and relief as they checked in for their return flights home.

The roar of rolling suitcases, the distant tannoy announcements and the thrum of chatter filled the air. I dodged through them all, my hand clutching my travel documents tightly. It was more than just a boarding pass to the US; it was the ticket to my future. The glimmer of hope for the life Cali and I would build together.

I tentatively joined the throngs that surrounded the confusing information boards, as I tried to navigate my way through to the gate, anxious I would get lost amid the chaos and miss my flight. My temples throbbed as I headed for my flight's check-in gate, irritated by the bustling crowds that would obstruct my linear path. A businessman, glued to his phone, bumped straight into me, causing my documents to fly out of my hand and flutter to the floor.

He scowled at me as I scrambled on the floor to retrieve them, slowing him down. He was not the only rude traveler I had encountered, but I tried to keep calm and push forward, I would not exert unnecessary energy on them, reserving every last bit for when I finally had Cali in my arms once more.

The sights and sounds of the airport were new and overwhelming, yet I persevered knowing I would walk through the fiery depths of Hell to reach her if necessary. All I could think about was that Cali needed me and I needed her. My mind recalled her words over and over in my mind. *"I'm pregnant."*

I took my cramped seat, and then sent Cali a quick text message as promised. I heard the flight attendant's voice drone on in the background, but was unable to hear a word she was saying. My mind was with Cali in the US, imagining the tiny life developing inside her, of what the future would hold for the three of us.

Anxiety gripped me as we flew high among the clouds, only settling when the plane finally touched back down onto the tarmac on US soil. The screen inside the headrest showed 08:45 yet it had been late afternoon when the plane had departed from Rhodes. For the whole flight I had not been able to think of anything other than her and of the child she carried in her womb.

After Lara and Eve's death, I never wanted to replace them, but meeting Cali had taken my world by storm, evoking feelings that I had no control of. This opportunity to have a life and a family with Cali was what I wanted. Embracing Cali's news was not an act of forgetting them, it was an acceptance that I could live the rest of my life with happiness and love in my heart.

I truly believed Aphrodite had smiled upon us, *how else could such a miracle be explained?* She had approved of our union, and blessed Cali with a child she believed she could never have.

I barely noticed the inside of the airport as I maneuvered through it, following the sign that marked 'Exit' with a scrunched-up piece of paper balled in my hand.

I sighed, glancing at my watch. "We are going to be late."

Twenty-Five

Nico

Cali stood out among the small congregation like a ray of sunshine on this dark and gloomy day. Dressed in a pale lemon dress, among the sea of black, she matched the singular rose clutched in her hand. But my eyes were drawn to her other hand, the one placed subconsciously on her flat stomach, a protective gesture over the new life that was growing inside of her.

I longed to be at her side, but this was her time to mourn, uninterrupted and free from distractions. So, I chose to watch the service from afar, not only for her privacy to grieve, but because it was too raw, even these many years later, to the memorial service held for my wife and daughter.

As I leaned against the great oak tree, hearing the birds chirp merrily from their nests as I felt the dull ache of my loss. My hands instinctively balled into fists; even though I had let go of the ghosts of my past, the pain will never truly go away. Time is said to be the greatest healer, but that is only because with time, memories fade and new ones are formed. I smiled as I gazed at her, *while I never want to forget them, Cali is my future now.*

She looked similar to the first time I saw her: wearing a similar yellow dress, filling my life with a brightness I never knew would be possible. That day, I could tell she was special, but there was no telling back then just how much she would change my life.

I felt a strong, masculine hand rest on my shoulder, knowing who it was before I turned around. It was the person who had always been my rock of unwavering support and wisdom, even when I did not deserve it. Andreas looked at me through watery eyes, a small smile on his face. "You should join us, Nico" He said, a small smile on his face as his eyes studied my face.

"I will..." I smiled back. "I'm just giving Cali the time and space she needs for this moment."

Andreas straightened his black tie, his own yellow rose in his other hand. "Thank you, aderfos mou, *my brother,* for persuading me to come."

With slow, purposeful steps Andreas joined the congregation, and I watched as her eyes lit up at the sight of him. Cali's arms wrapped around him, her shoulders shaking as she sobbed on his shoulder.

Andreas whispered something in her ear, which made her look over in my direction. She nodded her head slowly before pulling apart from Andreas. I could see her staring at me - even from this distance, I knew she was smiling.

Cali

All morning the rain had been relentless, thick heavy drops smattered the windscreen of the limousine as we followed the hearse to the church. The polished stone of the rain-drenched buildings reached up to the gloomy sky above, making it difficult to see where one finished and the other began. The only pop of color on this melancholy day was the flowers that adorned my mother's coffin, and the dress I wore.

Yellow had always been my mother's favorite color. *"It can cheer me up even on my darkest days,"* she once said. It seemed fitting to incorporate it into her funeral arrangements, from the yellow roses, to the yellow dress suit she was buried in, and the yellow dress I wore to match. She had always wanted her life to be celebrated as opposed to her death being mourned.

Fighting back tears, her words echoed in my mind. *"Everything that lives must die one day, Cali. The trick is to not waste a single moment of life while we still have it."* She had said those words a few days before my wedding as I sat beside her instead of ensuring all the final details were in place.

At the time, I interpreted her words as an encouragement to fully embrace my wedding, to appreciate the love I shared with Adam, and to savor every moment with him. But looking back, it was evident that her message carried a more prophetic meaning.

I smiled to myself as I reflected on her words. *I had not wasted a single moment when in Rhodes.* The whirlwind romance that had taken my breath away and had left me with the greatest surprise I had never imagined possible. *A real love and a child.*

The rain eased and small rays of sun filtered through the unhappy clouds, glinting on her polished oak casket as they lifted it out of the hearse, seeming to follow them as they marched towards her graveside.

Black umbrellas at the ready, the congregation filed around the open grave, just as Andreas arrived. I thought he would not come; my heart swelled at the sight of him. "Andreas! Thank you for coming, it truly means so much that you have made it." I gasped as my arms wrapped around him.

"Cali." He sighed, leaning into the embrace. "Nico is here too."

My eyes scanned the outskirts of the cemetery, looking for any sign of him, my heart racing and my stomach tightening into knots.

"He is leaning against the oak tree." Andreas chuckled softly, noticing my frantic search for him.

My eyes darted in his direction, spotting his recognizable silhouette anywhere; tall, broad-shouldered and muscular, just as the priest began to utter the Lord's Prayer. I smiled, though I doubted he could see it from this distance.

"Our Father who art in heaven, hallowed be thy name..."

The words seemed distant as I gazed down at her casket, her resting place forever beside my father. They held a *true* love - a resilient, affectionate love for each other that I had always admired. I thought I had found a similar love when I met Adam. A warmth flooded through me as I reminisced about my mom's clear dislike for him; even when we announced our engagement, I could see in her eyes that she *knew* he was no good for me. *I wonder what she would have thought of Nico...*

My hand fluttered to my stomach, remembering her encouraging words throughout mine and Adam's failed attempts to have a child, "I wish you had been able to meet each other." I whispered, as flashbacks of my own childhood played through my mind. Every last one filled with joy and genuine happiness as my parents held hands in the background.

"May your love transcend your lives on Earth and continue for all eternity... Amen."

"Amen."

My eyes snapped up, realizing that the casket had already been lowered, and the congregation had already placed their flowers inside the grave - they were all waiting for me. The rose clutched in my trembling hands, a thorn pricked my finger, instantly drawing blood. I winced, taking a few tentative steps forward. *I am not ready to say goodbye.*

My pulse quickened as fingers slid into the gaps of my own, calloused and rough from a life of manual labor. My instant reaction was to grasp them firmly, inhaling the familiar scent of vanilla and sandalwood as he stood beside me. "Cali, I'm right here." Nico whispered as his lips planted a kiss on my temple.

Each step toward the grave was harder than the last, my legs felt heavy, knowing that when I reached the edge, it would be my time to say goodbye. It would cement the reality that my mom was *never* coming back. Sobs swelled in my chest, pushing all the air out of my lungs. Trying to take deep breaths as I stared down into the pit, seeing the casket sitting at the bottom.

I clung onto Nico's hand even tighter as my other hand let go of the rose. It flitted down to the casket, some of its petals came loose and fluttered softly like confetti. *"Be happy Cali,"* I imagined my mom's voice telling me. *"Enjoy the ones you love while you can."*

I threw my arms around Nico as I sobbed; trying to will them into happy tears instead of sorrow. I was not sure how long we had stood like that for, but when I pulled away from him, the congregation and the priest had gone. We were all alone.

I looked into his caramel eyes, "Nico, I- I." His lips silenced me, as his fingertips danced on my stomach. It was still too early for a bump but the gesture made my skin tingle and my breaths came in quick, shallow pants. It was clear he too wanted this child; a child I never thought I would have been blessed with.

Tears streamed down my face as I kissed him once more, tasting the mint on his breath as my tongue sought his. I held onto him with every ounce of strength I could muster. "Thank you." I murmured.

Heavy rapid thuds vibrated through his chest as he held my body close to his. "Please come back to Rhodes with me," he urged, "let's go home."

I nodded slowly, "wherever you are is where I want to be."

In an instant, he lifted me off my feet and spun me around. The world whizzed by in a blur, but his face had remained the one consistent thing to look at. When he put me down, our bodies remained close, our foreheads pressed together. Nico's eyes locked onto mine and spoke in a low, solemn whisper. "Please never leave me again."

I felt the sun's rays upon my skin as it poked through the clouds once more, beaming down brilliantly on the two of us. The heat matched the warmth that radiated from my heart. "I have no intention of going anywhere without you, Nico."

Epilogue

***Nico** - Five years later.*

I gazed at the sandcastles, each one a poignant reminder of how much my life has changed since Cali had entered it. They were perfectly formed and intricately detailed, each one a blessing to behold.

My gaze surpassed them to the calm ocean waves in the distance, their hiss carried memories of what I had lost all those years ago. The more I watched the gentle ripples the deeper into thought I sank, almost as deep as Lara and Eve's watery graves.

Every wave that washed against the shore resembled their hands trying to claw their way out of them. I could feel the goosebumps prick my skin as the memory of that day played out in my mind. *Walls of flames, acrid black smoke, the ash that fell from the sky like snow.*

Out of the corner of my eye I could see my personal ray of sunshine, the reason for my happiness, the person who kept me afloat when the darkness of my sorrows threatened to drown me. Cali.

She was wearing the yellow sundress that I loved, with our five-year-old son Rocco clutching her hand. The sight of them both, so perfect and happy as they carried their buckets and spades towards me on the beach.

"Daddy!" Rocco shrieked as he ran over to me, his small arms stretching to wrap around my waist. "Are you going to help me and mommy?" His eyes lit up in excitement when I nodded my head.

"Of course, son." I chuckled, tousling his black curly locks. He bore more a resemblance to Cali, with his hair and his olive skin and his dark chocolate eyes. The only traits he seemed to have inherited from me was his sharp jaw and prominent brow.

There was something so pure and wholesome as I watched them build more castles by my feet.

"I'm going to look for shells!" Rocco shrieked, bouncing up and down like a ball of buzzing energy.

Cali's laughter filled the air, as we both watched him run along the soft white sand, picking only the prettiest shells to use for his sandcastle. My eyes watched him like a hawk, trying to ignore the tranquil waves that served as a warning that I had once failed once to protect the ones I loved.

Cali's hand rested on my thigh, her eyes now studying my profile, refusing to let Rocco out of my sight. "Nico," she murmured. "It's okay, you know, to feel sad, but never underestimate what an amazing father and *husband* you are."

Her lips brushed against my cheek before resting her head on my shoulders, the sorrow that lay heavy on my chest eased as my lungs filled with the scent of lavender and floral perfume. *I never thought I would ever be this happy again,* I thought as we helped Rocco place the shells on his sandcastle, watching his grin spread from ear to ear when it was complete.

"Rocco! Shall we go for pizza and ice cream?" Andreas' voice called from behind us. Bucket and spade abandoned, Rocco's legs couldn't get him to Andreas' side fast enough. He got halfway before running back over to us, embracing us once more.

"Bye mommy, bye daddy!"

Now that Andreas had semi-retired, he was more than happy to babysit Rocco so that Cali and I could just have some time alone together. To be a couple as well as parents. *"It is important that you still see each other as lovers, to keep that spark alive."* He had smirked the first time he had offered to look after Rocco overnight.

As our fingers interlocked, both of us watching Andreas and Rocco walk away in the distance, the atmosphere between us was intense, as it always was whenever we were alone. Still able to arouse me with the smallest of gestures, as it had been when we first met. Cali slid closer to me, her breathing hot against my neck as her lips grazed my collarbone. "Do you want to stay and watch the last of the sunset?" she asked.

The sun had almost fully disappeared under the line of the horizon, the sky indigo with flashes of crimson and magenta, coating the world below in its ethereal glow. I turned to face Cali, noticing how radiant her skin was and how full her breasts looked as my lips danced over her body.

My ears pricked, in the distance there was a voice, softer than a whisper, singing a child's lullaby; Eve's favorite. *Lullaby and good night, with roses bedight... Creep into thy bed, there pillow thy head. If God will thou shalt wake, when the morning doth break."*

Cali's playful attitude pushed aside the memories that tried to stir in my mind as she pulled herself on top of my lap, straddling me as my cock throbbed against her. She ground her hips against mine. Using her breasts to her advantage she pinned me down against the soft sand. destroying several sandcastles as she did so.

I looked at her with false shock, but she shrugged and a smirk appeared on her face. "I thought we could have some fun knocking them down for once" she said with a wink, "besides we can always rebuild them tomorrow." Her teeth grazed my bottom lip and desire oozed from her pores. "We have the rest of our lives to build sandcastles upon these shores, *together*."

My heart thumped uncontrollably being caught between her clenched thighs, unable to stop her as she ground herself against my unyielding shaft, thrusting her delicious nipples into my hungry mouth. I could never get enough of her, stealing moments like these as if we were horny teenagers, she brought the fun and the youth back into my life. *I would be lost without her.*

Cali unzipped my shorts, releasing my shaft from its confines. I groaned as her lips encircled my shaft, her tongue teasing the tip. Tendrils of her hair slipped through my fingers as I clutched at it, guiding her head deeper until my full length was consumed.

"Oh, Thea." I purred, as her mouth slid along my cock, feeling it twitch as Cali displayed her oral prowess. "I love you."

"I love you too" she whispered, as she allowed me to pull her dress over her head, revealing her naked body to me. "I need you Nico" she panted, slowly lowering herself onto me, enveloping my shaft with her warmth. Unable to control her burning lust she drove herself down on my cock, riding me hard and fast until our moans drifted in the sea breeze in perfect harmony.

I looked at her, this goddess, mine to love in every way. She took my breath away, with every stride, every moan and every sway of her hips.

As we frolicked in the sand, we destroyed more and more sandcastles, leaving nothing but piles of white sand in our wake. We giggled like children as we watched them crumble beneath our throes of passion.

I needed Cali in so many ways, grateful for her sudden arrival in my life to help me move on; my reason for waking up every morning - to love and cherish her as I had vowed.

"Nico..." she gasped, as she collapsed in the sand beside me, her head placed on my chest, her naked body glowed iridescent under the silver moon. I watched as her chest heaved as she recovered from her climax. Her body seemed different, thicker than before. Triggering a memory in my mind from the first time we had made love not long after her return to the island.

"Cali... are you?" My eyes glinted as they lingered on her stomach; my voice barely a whisper.

She nodded, unable to keep her smile under control any longer. I pulled her face up to mine, kissing her with a passion so fierce it consumed me. My hands explored her stomach, covering hers as they rested on her stomach; Aphrodite had blessed us once more.

"Lullaby and good night, those blue eyes close tight. Bright angels are near, so sleep without fear."

I recognized the voice that floated on the sea breeze, it sent a chill along my spine. Cali's eyes snapped up to my face, feeling my muscles tense as they embraced her. "Nico, what's wrong?"

I shook my head, trying to block out the singing that rang in my ears. "Nothing *Thea*," I said with a small smile as I pulled on my shorts and got to my feet. "This is *amazing* news."

I offered Cali my outstretched hand and helped her stand, my hands guiding her dress back over her glowing body. "I- I was going to tell you tomorrow... I know how hard this day is for you," she sighed.

I glanced at the sea behind us, at the sandcastles flattened at our feet and smiled while butterflies in my stomach flitted around uncontrollably. *She is so sexy when she is pregnant, and she is always horny as hell.*

Hand-in-hand we walked along the sleeping street, the amber glow of the streetlights cast an eerie glow. During the day the seafront was a thrum of activity, yet under the cover of darkness this part became a ghost town as tourists who wanted to party filled the nightclubs.

Our feet kicked up sand debris that had been scattered by the wind throughout the day, the soft crunch was the only sound that could be heard as we continued to walk.

I looked across at Cali about to speak when a reflection caught my eye in the darkened shop window. I looked over my shoulder expecting to see someone, to see *her*. But the street was just as deserted as it had been moments ago.

I tried not to keep searching, trying to ignore the feeling of being followed, but I knew what I saw; the shadow of a small girl in a flowing dress and curls that bounced behind her. I knew it was *Eve*.

A strong gust of wind whipped Cali's hair in all directions, carrying Eve's melodic voice as she continued to sing the last few lines of the lullaby. Each word dripped in sadness rather than the love and affection Lara did as she sang and cradled Eve in her arms.

"They will guard thee from harm, with fair dreamland's sweet charm."

The words were innocent, supposed to be soothing and comforting. But as the words continued to echo in my mind, I heard the undertones of Eve's relentless lament. She was sending me a subtle reminder of my failure to save them all those years ago. Feeding my doubts that I may not be able to protect the family I loved and cherished now.

"Lullaby and good night, those blue eyes close tight. Bright angels are near, so sleep without fear."

www.ingramcontent.com/pod-product-compliance
Ingram Content Group UK Ltd.
Pitfield, Milton Keynes, MK11 3LW, UK
UKHW022127211224
452733UK00013B/830